CONTENTS

A FEAST OF FOOTBALL

Do you remember your first football hero?

Do you remember the first game you went to watch?

Who is the player you will never forget? Or which goal is embedded in your brain forever?

We all have great football memories dating back from the current day to when we were much younger.

Can you remember England at Italia 90? Maybe our Classic Images - the likes of Maradona's Hand of God goal, or Gazza's tears - will jog your football memories.

Perhaps it's reading about the current stars and the ones who could be the legends of the future that will give you a kick.

One thing is for certain: If you like football you will love this book of the beautiful game.

We've dug into Shoot's archives that date back to 1969 to bring you some fantastic memories of the past.

We've also included some more recent features and interviews, plus there are some totally new articles and interviews written especially for this book. And there are some great images that have never been seen before!

We hope you enjoy!

Published by Pedigree Books Ltd.
Published 2010.

PEDIGREE BOOKS, BEECH HILL HOUSE,
WALNUT GARDENS, EXETER, DEVON EX4 4DH
shoot@pedigreegroup.co.uk

EDITOR COLIN MITCHELL
DEPUTY EDITOR LEE PRICE
DESIGN STUART BIRTLES
AND JONATHAN FINCH

RED HOT ROONEY

There can't be a player or fan on the planet who doesn't appreciate the skills of Wayne Rooney.

In the space of just over eight years the lad from the backstreets of Liverpool has risen to become one of the top stars of world football.

Yet the down-to-earth Scouser is still just 25-years-old and his best years could still be ahead of him.

The goals rush he enjoyed during season 2009-10, when he hit 34 in 44 games for Manchester United, and a further nine for England during qualification for World Cup 2010 catapulted him up the world rankings.

His all-action style, non-stop running and the addition of those vitals goals meant Old Trafford fans quickly forgot about the departure of £80m superstar Cristiano Ronaldo.

And England fans know that without the bustling forward their international hopes are that much weaker too.

It's not a great distance from his home town to Manchester but Wayne Rooney has come a long way in terms of his skills and the development of his game.

"When I was 16 I had no fear whatsoever," says Wayne. "I do think about the game a lot more now and the bigger the match the more responsibility I feel.

"I must keep on trying to continue what I'm doing, practising all the time and help the team to improve."

And it's the words of one of his former Everton colleagues that still ring in his ears: "I always remember Alan Stubbs telling me to try and enjoy the career because it goes quicker than you think. It has flown by and I just want to try and enjoy every season as much as I can before it is over."

ⓘ FACT FILE

WAYNE MARK ROONEY

BIRTH DATE: October 24, 1985

BIRTH PLACE: Croxteth, Liverpool

POSITION: Striker

HEIGHT: 1.78m (5ft 10in)

CLUBS: Everton, Manchester United

INTERNATIONAL: England (60 caps, 25 goals)

DID YOU KNOW?
Wayne and wife Coleen had their first child – son Kai Wayne Rooney – on November 2, 2009. Dad took his son on the pitch after the last game of the season.

MAN OF THE MOMENT

SKILL FACTOR

Playing at Manchester United with their galaxy of stars has undoubtedly helped The Roonster who hopes to emulate one of his team-mates and friends.

"The number of games Giggsy has played is unbelievable," he admits.

"I have always said I would love to end my career here and if I can get anywhere near Giggsy it would be an amazing achievement. You have to have great respect for him."

Ryan Giggs is rightly praised for his ability on the wing and, in more recent times, creativity in the centre of the park. Wayne plays down his own abilities...

"I never really try skills. If it happens it happens. I find it works better if I don't think about it. I certainly don't look Brazilian and I can't dance like them either," he smiles.

So how come there was a rush of goals? "Now I am getting into the box it is easier to score," says Wayne.

"We have been working on that at United for a few years. I had been dropping deep and probably trying to play players rather than getting into the box."

Ryan Giggs is like the Duracell bunny... he just keeps going!

MR DEPEN

FACT FILE

Birth date:
November 29, 1973

Birth place:
Cardiff

Position:
Midfielder

Clubs:
Manchester United

International:
Wales (64 caps, 12 goals)

Did you know?
In May 2008 Ryan passed the 758 game mark for Man United making him the club's record appearance holder of all time.

At the age of 37 most Premier League players have hung up their boots. Most will not have stayed loyal and played for just one top-class club all of their career.

But Ryan Giggs will still be in the famous red shirt of Man United at that age - as he has been every year since her turned professional.

The tricky winger has been around at Old Trafford since the season before the Premier League began - and until the start of season 2010-11 was the only player to have turned out AND scored every season in the competition started in 1992-93.

As other players have fallen by the wayside or retired gracefully, Giggsy has just kept on going, often looking as though he was improving with age.

He was inducted into the Football Hall of Fame four years ago and is the player with the most top-flight titles to his name, 11 in total.

What his boss says

Sir Alex Ferguson who has been at Man United even longer than Giggsy: "Ryan is exceptionally fit. We just have to keep him fresh and make sure he has the motivation because I want him to continue. He is a fantastic person to have about the place. The experience he brings is invaluable. There are certain types of people you only get once in a lifetime. Ryan is a complete one-off."

RYAN GIGGS ON...

Goal celebrations
"When you score a goal, especially an important one, the feelings rise up and you've got no control over yourself. That's what football is all about. You never know what is going to happen next."

Keeping his career going
"Different things have inspired me over the years, seeing players like Cristiano Ronaldo come through, Raphael now - when you see him bombing past you have to do something about that. You have to raise your game."

Representing Wales
"It is a big disappointment that I never experienced playing for Wales in a World Cup. But I wouldn't change my career. I've had a great one and never imagined it would be like this."

Reaching the first-team
"Bryan Robson was an old man to me when I made my debut - now I am older than he was when I got into the team! I can't even remember anything about my debut [against Everton, March 2 1991, as a sub]."

Sir Alex Ferguson
"The manager knows me better than anyone. He has seen me almost every day for 20 years and he knows how to handle me. He's a master at handling players. If you aren't doing what he feels you should be doing he tells you, no matter how old you are."

Taking on Europe
"It is hard work winning the Champions League. Mentally and physically it is draining you must have the desire and hunger."

DABLE

The 1st. part
of a special interview with
GEORGE BEST

GEORGE Best has had headlines stretching miles and miles written about his remarkable career. And despite his spectacular, crowd-pleasing talents out on the park, many of the eye-catching banners have been far from complimentary.

An Irishman blessed with the gift of the gab as well as fantastic soccer skill, he's had more than his fair share of trouble.

His disciplinary record is bad, with most of his bookings or sendings-off being for what he said, rather than what he did. As was his recent sensational dismissal at Southampton, following a war of words with referee Les Shapter.

He's been called "a stupid fool" for getting into so much trouble. For getting involved in arguments with referees. Manchester United fans

'I became bored at Man. United'

for a while hated him for walking out on the club — but the hate turned to adoration when he returned to the fold. Until, finally, he quit the Manchester scene altogether.

Best, 33 caps for Northern Ireland, played 361 League games for Manchester United and scored 137 League goals. He turned on abundant skills to help United become the first English club to win the European Cup.

And he left the Old Trafford club after a New Year's Day game at Loftus Road when United, at the bottom end of the table, lost 3-0 to Queens Park Rangers — and Bestie looked . . . just lost!

A brilliant, world-class player had apparently blown out his career years early. For a long time after that January 1, 1974, game in West London he played only Sunday

friendlies — and claimed he didn't miss the game at all.

That could have been true but there is no doubt that millions of soccer fans found they missed Georgie Best . : .

Then, after a summer in the North American Soccer League, he signed for Fulham for this season. With Rodney Marsh, who started his League career with Fulham before moving on to Q.P.R. and then Manchester City before also hitting the United States trail, Bestie became once again a hero figure.

A home game against Bristol Rovers. And Bestie had the ball in the Rovers net after 71 seconds precisely. What's more, he could have had two other goals if luck had gone his way. His crowd-pulling ability was as sharp as ever, with a gate of 21,127 exactly — or around

130 percent up on the corresponding game the previous season. Actual receipts were 300 percent up.

Now it's George, 30, talking about the fairy-tale comeback, and his hang-ups and his secret wishes.

First, as he sits relaxed and smiling, he says: "When I knew I was being allowed to play in the Football League again I was over the moon. It made a perfect ending to what had been a bad period of my life. Yet just being part of a League club wasn't the end of it — I had to prove myself. I knew that, for lots of fans, I was G. Best, former star, now very much on trial for his footballing life.

"I can understand people thinking this was just another comeback by a player who had earlier done all the wrong things. Some writers said

that I'd be okay as long as I wasn't bored with the game. Their bet was that I'd be bored pretty quickly.

"But I know more about me than they do. I'd made comebacks galore before, and I accept that. But they had all been with the same club, Manchester United.

"It was a club with tradition and I felt that some things were not right there and — well, yes, I got bored. Though I've kicked a football around since I was just 18 months old, and love the game, I was quite happy to get out of it.

"Yet when I went to America I felt the old enthusiasm coming back. I knew that I wanted to be part of the English scene again. And instead of making my umpteenth comeback with United, I went to a completely new set-up. For me, Fulham is a great club."

Best is full of praise for the other players at Craven Cottage. It's no secret that some of them were not so sure about the arrival of the Belfast boyo, specially as he was apparently being paid a lot of money for his services.

One player, who should remain nameless, said: "He won't work for us. Not unless we give him his own ball to play with."

'MY

Former Man United star George Best explains his move to Fulham

But through long, strenuous training sessions, Georgie proved he was determined to find fitness as soon as possible. He knew he could play in short sharp bursts, as he had in America, but he started looking for 90-minute fitness.

He says now: "I know better than most that football is a team game. Take Fulham. It was great to return to England and see Bobby Moore playing with so much commanding skill at the back.

"He can control things brilliantly. And John Mitchell, who knows how to score goals, is another fine player, learning all the time and a Londoner through and through.

"There are others. There's Les Barrett, a long-term servant of the club, with well over 400 League

club is definitely going to make progress. No argument."

Best accepts that he is a marked man in terms of crowd reaction away from home — and from opponents whether it is home or away.

"Take the people who love to come and boo me. I can't complain. It's their right, and they pay through the turnstile for the privilege. But I can't let it affect me. There is one way to silence the boo-merchants and that is to get in a winning position.

"Our gate receipts and attendance figures show that people want to see our kind of show, Rodney and myself. Incidentally Rodney Marsh is tremendous. The things he does out there on the park just defy description.

"A couple of the goals he's scored this season have been as good as I've seen anywhere, specially the second one against Hereford at the Cottage — though I must say the one I got against Peterborough away from home was a little Irish gem.

"Rodney and I have a remarkable understanding. I know that some purists must have been annoyed when, against Hereford, he came back and actually tackled me to get the ball — but remember we were well ahead at the time and weren't taking any risks.

"Now things are going well, except that I obviously still have to learn to keep my mouth shut when I feel outraged about things that happen on the park. I'm always talking my way into trouble and when you think of the people who kick other people around and get away with it, then it seems a little bit unfair.

"I've got to bear in mind all the time that I am George Best, and that people think I'm something special. I don't feel all that special when a game is under way. I'd rather be one of a team. But it's obvious that I'm always going to be

'I have to learn to keep my mouth shut'

'COMEBACK...'

'Fulham is a great club'

games to his credit. Now he just has to be one of the best wingers in the business. He's scored his fair share of goals, too.

"As for John Evanson — well, I heard our coach Bobby Campbell saying that Evanson just has to be the best free-transfer player ever. I'll go along with that.

"Then there is the club-captain, Alan Slough. He's very much on my side. I've had a couple of bits of trouble since I came back, but Alan knows what it is all about and he does his best, as skipper, to protect me. He's very involved in the coaching side of the game as well, and that is another bonus."

And Best said: "No point running through the whole team. Fulham has the right blend of talent and the

picked out."

Suddenly George Best went very straightfaced indeed. He said: "I'll be disappointed if I don't score around 20 goals this season. When I was in America this summer, I worked really hard to get my weight down and get fit.

"I knew all the time that I couldn't give up football. In the States, I hit 15 goals in 23 games. I'd had a couple of terrible years, but I wanted to remind people of the 12 years when I did things right."

But Best still has one regret, and several ambitions, and at least one good idea, he thinks, to make football even more attractive. He'll explain in detail next week.

MARADONA WORLD CUP 1986

You will remember this game best for Maradona's infamous 'Hand of God' goal against England. This is his second and equally outrageous strike in that game. After waltzing passed the England defence as if the players weren't there - thanks to his skill rather than their lack of it - the Argentina forward slotted the ball past keeper Peter Shilton. England defender Terry Butcher later admitted to **Shoot** that he would have taken out Maradona - if he could have got close enough!

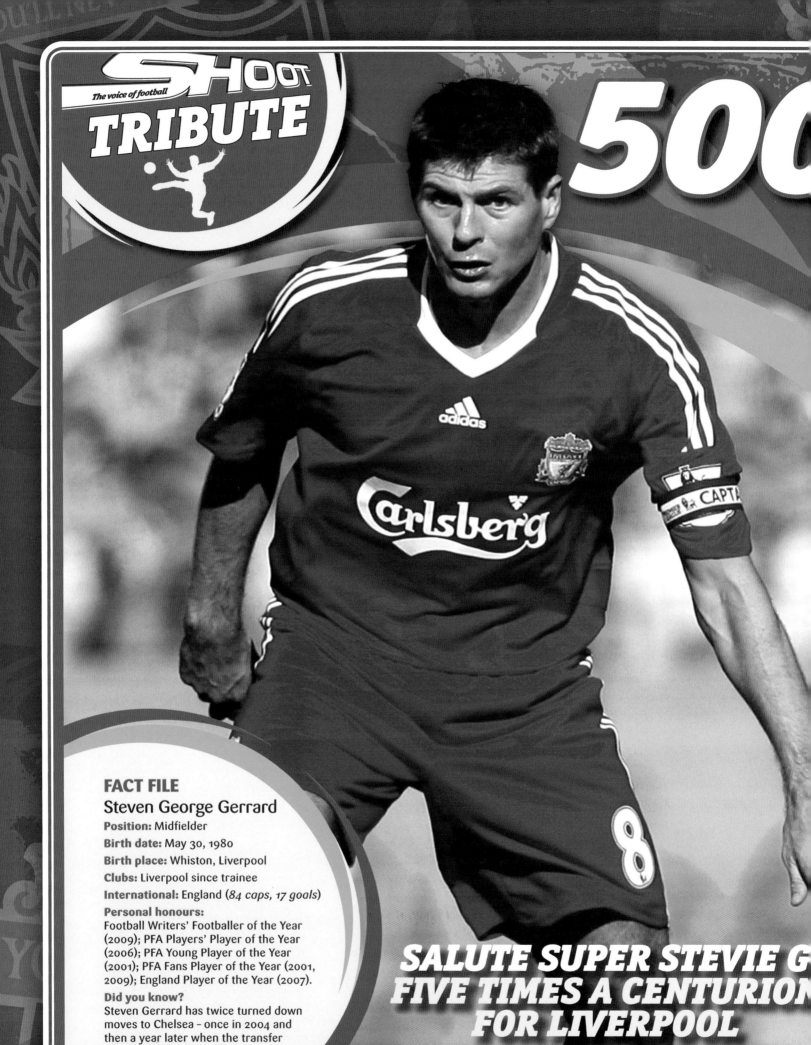

500

FACT FILE

Steven George Gerrard

Position: Midfielder

Birth date: May 30, 1980

Birth place: Whiston, Liverpool

Clubs: Liverpool since trainee

International: England (*84 caps, 17 goals*)

Personal honours:
Football Writers' Footballer of the Year (2009); PFA Players' Player of the Year (2006); PFA Young Player of the Year (2001); PFA Fans Player of the Year (2001, 2009); England Player of the Year (2007).

Did you know?
Steven Gerrard has twice turned down moves to Chelsea - once in 2004 and then a year later when the transfer appeared to done and dusted.

SALUTE SUPER STEVIE G
FIVE TIMES A CENTURION
FOR LIVERPOOL

NOT OUT!

Steven Gerrard's 500th Reds Appearance
Blackburn Rovers v Liverpool , December 5, 2009

"He has got the team playing without fear, without that weight of expectation on our shoulders. We will respect anyone we come up against but I think it's time other teams started fearing us."

What they said...

Rafa Benitez, former Liverpool manager:
"To reach 500 games for one club is remarkable. He is certainly one of the very best players I have ever worked with. Stevie is known as a top-class player all around the world."

Fernando Torres, Anfield team-mate:
"Stevie has had a lot of praise from some of the best players in the world, and that is quite right because I think he is the best in the world. He is a great team player but he can also win a game on his own when maybe we are not playing so well. I cannot think of a player I would rather be playing with."

Jamie Carragher, fellow Scouser at Liverpool:
"It's never a clever thing to write Stevie off because even when there are times when he doesn't play well, he will produce a goal."

Fabio Capello, England boss:
"He is at the very top of his game. You need players with humility and I think he has that. I think he is an important player for England, according to my plans."

Just over eight years ago, on the eve of the 2002 World Cup finals, Steven Gerrard was being touted as a key player for England.

His battling qualities had pushed the then 21-year-old to the fore and he was key to Sven Goran Eriksson's plans in Japan and South Korea.

Then disaster struck. The Liverpool midfielder, who had suffered a series of injuries related to growing pains, suffered a groin injury that was to cost him his place in the England squad.

It was feared that the problems could dog him through his career but medical experts came up with an answer and Stevie G's remarkable career was back on track.

Now the one-club Scouser has passed the 500 games mark for the Reds, the incredible milestone reaching in the goal-less draw against Blackburn in December 2009.

Stevie G's war cry

Fast forward to the 2010 World Cup finals and Stevie G captained his country as stand-in for the injured Rio Ferdinand.

Gerrard has admitted that this could well be his last appearance in the finals of the tournament but he entered the fray brimming with confidence, thanks to boss Fabio Capello.

"My form for England has improved since he came in. I have spoken to Fabio Capello about how to get the best out of me for England," admitted Stevie G.

GERRARD'S GREATEST MOMENTS

DEBUT
Gerrard came on as a last-minute substitute against Blackburn on November 29, 1998.

FIRST GOAL
His first goal for the first-team came in season 1999-2000 during a 4-1 victory over Sheffield Wednesday.

ENGLAND DEBUT
Gerrard made his international debut against Ukraine on May 31, 2000 after being called up by Kevin Keegan.

FIRST TROPHY
The 2001 League Cup thanks to a penalty shoot-out victory over Birmingham after a 1-1 draw.

LIVERPOOL CAPTAIN
Appointed in October 2003 by Gerard Houllier and retained as skipper by Rafa Benitez.

FIRST SENIOR ENGLAND GOAL
What a time to score! He got the first, the equaliser, in the 5-1 rout of Germany in a 2002 World Cup qualifier.

FA CUP FINAL
Two goals by Stevie G, both equalisers, in the FA Cup Final against West Ham, helped the Red Devils to a penalty shoot-out and another trophy in 2006.

EURO STAR
Stevie G made his 100th appearance in European club competitions for Liverpool on March 10, 2009. He scored twice in the 4-0 win against Real Madrid.

CHAMPIONS LEAGUE VICTORY
Gerrard scored one in Liverpool's dramatic comeback to 3-3 from 3-0 down against AC Milan. He didn't take part in the penalty shoot-out but was named Man of the Match.

HAT-TRICK
Last March, Gerrard scored his first-ever hat-trick in the Premier League during the 5-0 victory over Aston Villa.

400 GAMES
And he scored against Arsenal on October 28, 2007!

FOOTBALLER OF THE YEAR
The Football Writers gave Stevie G their award in 2009, the first Liverpool star to get the trophy since John Barnes in 1990.

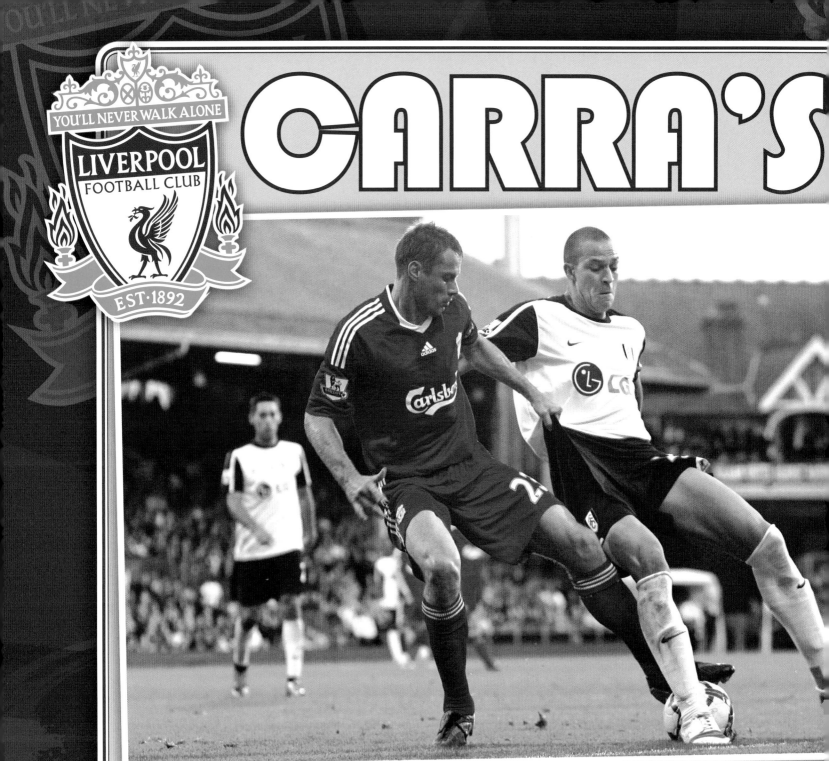

ℹ FACT FILE

JAMES CARRAGHER

BIRTH DATE: January 28, 1978

BIRTH PLACE: Bootle, Merseyside

POSITION: Striker

HEIGHT: 1.85m (6ft 1in)

CLUBS: None

INTERNATIONAL: England

DID YOU KNOW?
Carra's little boy James sports a Fernando Torres shirt and goes around their home singing the fans' chant about the Spain striker!

JAMIE CARRAGHER'S AMAZING WISH...

Jamie Carragher has a dream! Another Champions League victory for Liverpool? No! A first elusive Premier League title for Anfield? No!

The defender who passed the landmark figure of 600 games for the Merseysiders in 2010, wants one thing in the latter stages of his illustrious career – an appearance at Wembley.

Amazingly, until the start of the 2010-11 season the Liverpool stalwart has never appeared for his local club between the old Twin Towers or under the new sky-dominating Arch.

"I've been around for a long time but have not played at Wembley for Liverpool, only England,"he revealed "I've not even been to the cup semis at Wembley. I am desperate to get there. I've been too Cardiff a few times but I would love to get to Wembley, to take my son there."

Carra created another landmark in his remarkable carrer when he once again pulled on his international boots in 2010, three years after quitting the international scene.

He answered a call from Fabio Capello to help out England at the World Cup finals, even though he insisted that would definitely be the end of his international days.

DREAM

YOU'LL NEVER WALK ALONE

LIVERPOOL FOOTBALL CLUB
EST·1892

ℹ️ FACT FILE

ROY HODGSON

BIRTH DATE: August 9, 1947

BIRTH PLACE: Croydon, London

POSITION: Manager

CLUBS: Carshalton, Halmstad, Bristol City, Orebro, Malmo, Neuchatel Xamax, Switzerland, Inter, Blackburn, Grasshopper, Copenhagen, Udinese, UAE, Viking, Finland, Fulham, Liverpool

DID YOU KNOW?
Hodgson had a long and varied career as a non-league footballer, before briefly becoming a PE teacher.

HODGSON HOPES TO RETURN FORMER GLORIES TO ANFIELD

After the chaos that surrounded the back-end of Rafa Benitez's reign at Liverpool, the club looked to Mr Reliable, Roy Hodgson, to steady the ship.

He's gone about his job quietly, carefully weeding out some of Benitez's flops – Albert Riera for instance – while building his own side.

Clearly working on a budget, Hodgson has already made the clever signings of free agent Joe Cole, Christian Poulsen, who he worked with at Copenhagen; plus young Rangers defender Danny Wilson for just £2m.

Most importantly, perhaps, the wily manager has convinced Fernando Torres and Steven Gerrard that their futures are on Merseyside.

With the rise of Manchester City and Tottenham, the perennial outside bets of Aston Villa and Everton and the unpredictable nature of the Premier League, securing a Champions League return is a challenge in itself.

But Hodgson wants more than that. He recognises the great heritage of the club, and has insisted that he will be aiming to bring home silverware every season.

ROY-AL CHALLENGE

➜ TOP JOBS! HODGSON'S MANAGERIAL HISTORY

➜ SCANDINAVIAN SUCCESSES

Hodgson spent the first 13 years of his career in Sweden - except a four-month stint with Bristol City in 1982 - where he made a name for himself. Hodgson won two Swedish titles with Halmstads before his ill-fated spell in Bristol and claimed another two titles with Malmo after returning to Scandinavia. He also added two Swedish cups in his time with Malmo. After a decade working away from the area, Hodgson returned to Scandinavia with Copenhagen, winning the Danish double in his sole season at the helm.

➜ SWISS DREAMS

Hodgson took charge of Neuchatel Xamax in 1990, leading them to European victories over both Real Madrid and Celtic, impressing sufficiently to be poached by the Switzerland national side.

He took the Swiss to the 1994 World Cup finals, their first since 1966, and helped them to progress to the Round of 16 stage, including a draw against eventual finalists Italy. During his tenure the country reached a record high of third in the FIFA rankings. He later managed the national teams of Finland and the UAE.

➜ ITALY AND ENGLAND

His performances at an international level drew the attention of Inter Milan, who brought Hodgson in to rebuild their ailing side. He took them to the 1997 UEFA Cup Final before heading for Blackburn. That spell was short-lived, as was a subsequent reign at Udinese. His eventual arrival at Fulham saw him transform a relegation threatened outfit into Europa League finalists in the space of three seasons, earning him the move to Liverpool.

YOU'LL NEVER WALK ALONE

LIVERPOOL FOOTBALL CLUB

EST·1892

KING KENNY

'KING KENNY' WAS PIVOTAL IN THE APPOINTMENT OF ROY HODGSON TO THE ANFIELD HOT SEAT. WORKING TOGETHER, THE PAIR COULD WELL REINTRODUCE THE GLORY DAYS TO LIVERPOOL

22

Kenny Dalglish's glittering career at Liverpool earned him a display case full of silverware that includes seven league titles.

Arguably the finest player to strut his stuff in front of The Kop, the Scot also lifted three European Cups before taking over as player-manager at Anfield.

At the end of his first season in charge – 1985-86 – the forward had collected the Reds' first league and cup Double.

What made that success even sweeter was that Everton finished second in the league and were beaten by their Mersey rivals in the FA Cup Final.

Disaster struck when Liverpool were beaten in the 1988 Cup Final by Wimbledon but they recovered by again beating Everton in the final the following season.

When he quit Liverpool in 1991, Dalglish said he wanted a break from football, but months later the late Jack Walker, owner of Blackburn, talked the Scot into taking over at Ewood Park.

His first year saw Rovers promoted via the play-offs and then they landed the Premier League title in his third season.

After leaving Blackburn, where he had become director of football, Dalglish had another break from the game before taking over at Newcastle. He led the Geordies to second before being sacked.

A brief spell as Celtic director of football followed before Dalglish eventually returned to Liverpool in July 2009 as an ambassador and key member of their youth academy set-up.

➲ KENNY DALGLISH'S LIVERPOOL STATS

515 appearances, **172** goals
307 games as manager
8 League titles
2 FA Cups
3 European Cups
4 League Cups
1 European Super Cup
5 Charity Shields
1 FWA Footballer of the Year
1 PFA Player of the Year
3 Manager of the Year awards

Joe Cole was the stand-out player available on a Bosman free transfer during the summer of 2010.

After growing disillusioned with life at Chelsea, where he felt undervalued and underrated, Cole was linked with a move to the elite of English football.

Manchester United and Arsenal were suggested, but Champions League qualifiers Tottenham looked favourites, with Harry Redknapp feeling it was a done deal and a signing that could take Spurs to the next level.

It was a shock when London boy Cole turned his back on his roots and moved north to sign for Liverpool, who couldn't even offer him Champions League football.

Citing the club's proud heritage and tremendous winning record over the years, Cole insisted that he had signed for 'the biggest club in the world'.

Mesmerising with the ball at his feet, Cole's creativity has often been stifled in the past by being shipped out wide. Managers who couldn't handle his roaming style of play tried to restrict him to a disciplined role, diminishing his performances in the process.

Under new boss Roy Hodgson, Cole has been promised a more central role, his favoured position.

Undoubtedly a rare star player of natural ability, able to sprinkle a bit of magic on every game he appears in, this will be seen as Cole's last big chance to establish himself as the mercurial talent most fans expected to see develop over the past few season.

Edging closer to 30, Cole should be at his peak. Liverpool boast a solid core of players, which could allow their new signing the space and freedom he craves.

COLE AND THE GANG

Playmaker hopes to lead Liverpool renaissance

ℹ FACT FILE

JOSEPH JOHN COLE

BIRTH DATE: November 8, 1981
BIRTH PLACE: London, England
POSITION: Attacking midfielder
HEIGHT: 1.75m (5ft 9in)
CLUBS: West Ham United, Chelsea, Liverpool
INTERNATIONAL: England

DID YOU KNOW?
Cole shot to fame as a schoolboy, after grabbing seven of England youth's eight goals in a victory against Spain.

COLE'S CORKERS: New Liverpool ace's five best goals

➲ 1. ENGLAND v SWEDEN WORLD CUP 2006

After an England corner was headed to apparent safety, Cole coolly brought the ball down on his chest before unleashing a stunning, dipping volley from fully 30-yards, which beat the keeper all ends up.

➲ 2. CHELSEA v MAN UNITED 2006

A long goal kick upfield was flicked to Cole via the chest of Drogba, With three United defenders around him, the diminutive midfielder created some space for himself before smashing home to secure the league title.

➲ 3. CHELSEA v MAN UNITED 2010

Florent Malouda jinked down the left flank, dragging his pass across the face of goal. Cole, at the near post, nonchalantly backheeled the ball between the legs of Patrice Evra and beyond Edwin van der Sar.

➲ 4. CHELSEA v LIVERPOOL 2007

In an all-English Champions League semi-final, Cole gave Chelsea a 1-0 first leg victory, with one of the most important goals of his career. The Reds won the second leg by the same scoreline and prevailed on penalties, before being beaten by Milan in the final.

➲ 5. CHELSEA v TOTTENHAM 2008

Cole latched onto a Frank Lampard through ball brilliantly to beat a defender and slot Chelsea into a 4-3 lead. They couldn't hold out, and the game ended 4-4.

CLASSIC IMAGE

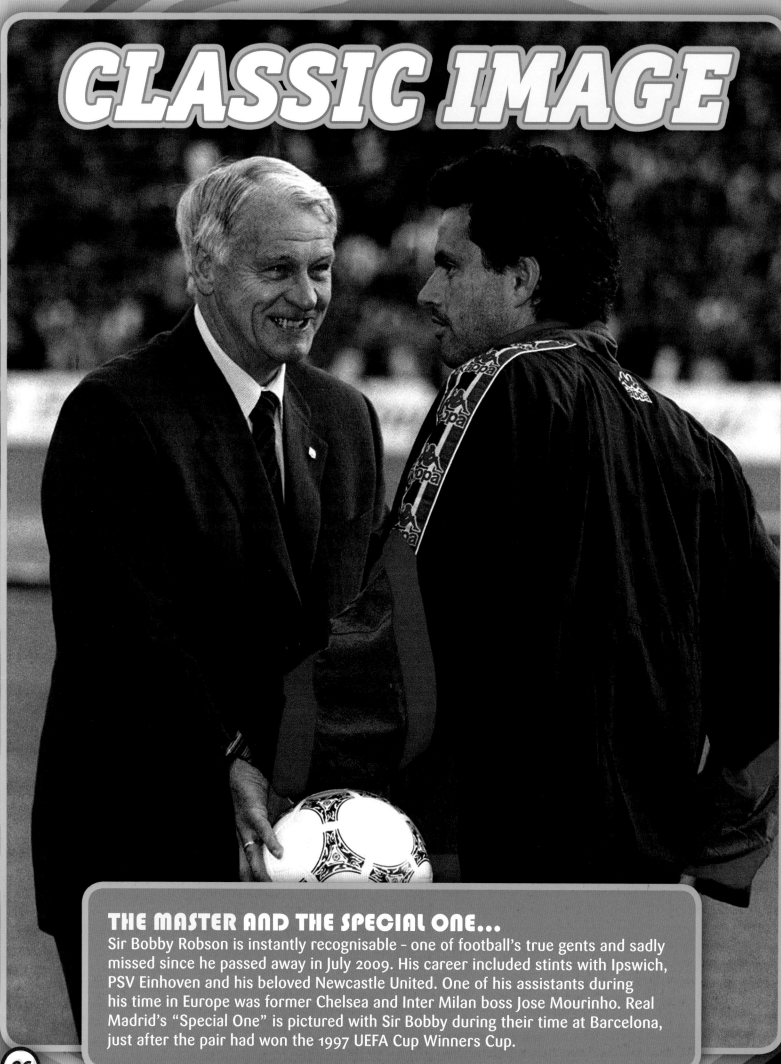

THE MASTER AND THE SPECIAL ONE...

Sir Bobby Robson is instantly recognisable - one of football's true gents and sadly missed since he passed away in July 2009. His career included stints with Ipswich, PSV Einhoven and his beloved Newcastle United. One of his assistants during his time in Europe was former Chelsea and Inter Milan boss Jose Mourinho. Real Madrid's "Special One" is pictured with Sir Bobby during their time at Barcelona, just after the pair had won the 1997 UEFA Cup Winners Cup.

LEGENDS!

The stars of today could be the legends of tomorrow. Here are some of the world's best from yester-year – and some of the current players are who are hoping to reach the same legendary status

Pele

Edison Arantes do Nascimento • **Birth date:** October 23, 1940
Birth place: Tres Coraoes, Brazil • **Position:** Forward
Clubs: Santos, New York Cosmos
International: Brazil (92 caps, 77 goals)
Now: Football ambassador

Many footballers who weren't even born when Pele was playing still rate him as their No.1 of all-time after watching him in action on film.

He scored an amazing 1,280 goals in 1,363 games - a record that has been rubber-stamped as official and is hardly likely to be beaten...ever!

Even a spell in Brazil's army never stopped Pele from playing and when you consider he was not an out-and-out striker his goal scoring record is even more incredible.

He would be regarded nowadays as an attacking midfielder or second striker but he could dribble tantalisingly, pass with accuracy, show a fast turn of speed and had lethal shooting and heading ability.

Pele hit 589 goals in his 605 league and cup games for Santos before his move to America where he notched another 64 goals in 107 games for New York.

THEN

BRAZIL

Kaka

Ricardo Izecson dos Santos Leite
Birth date: April 22, 1982 • **Birth place:** Brasilia, Brazil
Position: Midfielder
Clubs: Sao Paulo, AC Milan, Real Madrid
International: Brazil (82 caps, 27 goals)
Now: Real Madrid paid £56m for Kaka in June 2009.

Although he's regarded as one of the top players in the world there's still a feeling that Kaka is capable of hitting even greater heights.

He can use his immense skill level to influence games and utilise his strength to hold off challenges or hold up play.

He can make the game look easy, either scoring himself from range or with neat bits of skills or by creating chances for his team-mates.

The 2007 European and World Player of the Year was a Serie A and Champions League winner with AC Milan. He was also twice Serie A Footballer of the Year and a three-times winner of Foreign Footballer of the Year during his time in Italy.

Maradona

Diego Armando Maradona • **Birth date:** October 30, 1960
Birth place: Buenos Aries, Argentina • **Position:** Forward
Clubs: Argentinos Juniors, Boca Juniors, Barcelona, Napoli, Sevilla, Newell's Old Boys, Boca Juniors
International: Argentina (91 caps, 34 goals)
Now: Argentina coach

Maradona scored five goals in the 1986 World Cup finals as he captained his country to victory.

Two of those goals came against England in the quarter-finals. The first was his infamous "Hand of God" goal where he pushed the ball into the net with his hand. His second strike involved him running from his own half and past seven England players to score.

Just 5ft 5in tall, Maradona was deadly as an attacking midfielder or striker. Argentina's youngest international at the age of 16, he won two South America Player of the Year awards.

When he moved to Barcelona it was for a then world record £5m. He won La Liga, the league cup and Spanish Supercup at the Camp Nou in his first season.

Another world record £6.9m fee took him to Napoli where he enjoyed an Italian league and cup double, followed by the UEFA Cup and other silverware.

He appeared at the 1982, 1986, 1990 and 1994 World Cup finals, despite a 15-month ban in 1991 for failing a dope test.

THEN

ARGENTINA

Messi

Lionel Andres Messi • **Birth date:** June 24, 1987
Birth place: Rosaria, Argentina • **Position:** Winger
Clubs: Barcelona
International: Argentina (49 caps, 13 goals)
Now: Messi has played for Barcelona since 2003, when he was still just 16!

He's been compared to his legendary countryman Maradona and not just because he has scored a "Hand of God" goal and a wonder-strike very similar to the master!

Messi can play on either wing and is a creator as much as a scorer. He's loaded with natural skill and tricks and is a player who can get fans on the edge of their seats as they wait for moments of greatness.

It's hard to believe he is still only 23 and his best years should still be ahead of him.

The World and European Footballer of the Year in 2009, as well as the Player of the Champions League.

Top scorer in the Champions League in both 2009 and 2010, along with being La Liga's Player of the Year in both those years.

Four times Argentina's Player of the Year – in 2005, 2007, 2008 and 2009 – his trophy cabinet is already groaning under the weight of silverware.

NOW

Eusebio

Eusébio da Silva Ferreira • **Birth date:** January 25, 1942
Birth place: Mozambique • **Position:** Forward
Clubs: Sporting Marques, Benfica, Rhode Island Oceaneers, Boston Minutement, Monterrey, Beira-Mar, Toronto Metros, Las Vegas Quicksilvers, New Jersey Americans, Uniao de Tomar
International: Portugal (64 caps, 41 goals)
Now: Retired but still keeps links with the Portugal international side.

Top scorer with nine goals when the World Cup was staged in England, Eusebio endeared himself to fans all around the planet during Portugal's run to third in the 1966 finals.

His silky skills, speed and power allied to an incredible goal record made him one of the best players ever and one who will never be forgotten for his 15 years with Benfica – where he is still their record goalscorer – or for his 12 years serving Portugal.

A modest man, he has 11 Portuguese league titles to his credit, plus two European Cups. A bronze statue of him stands outside of Benfica's ground, there is another in America, and Tussauds created a wax model of the man.

THEN

PORTUGAL

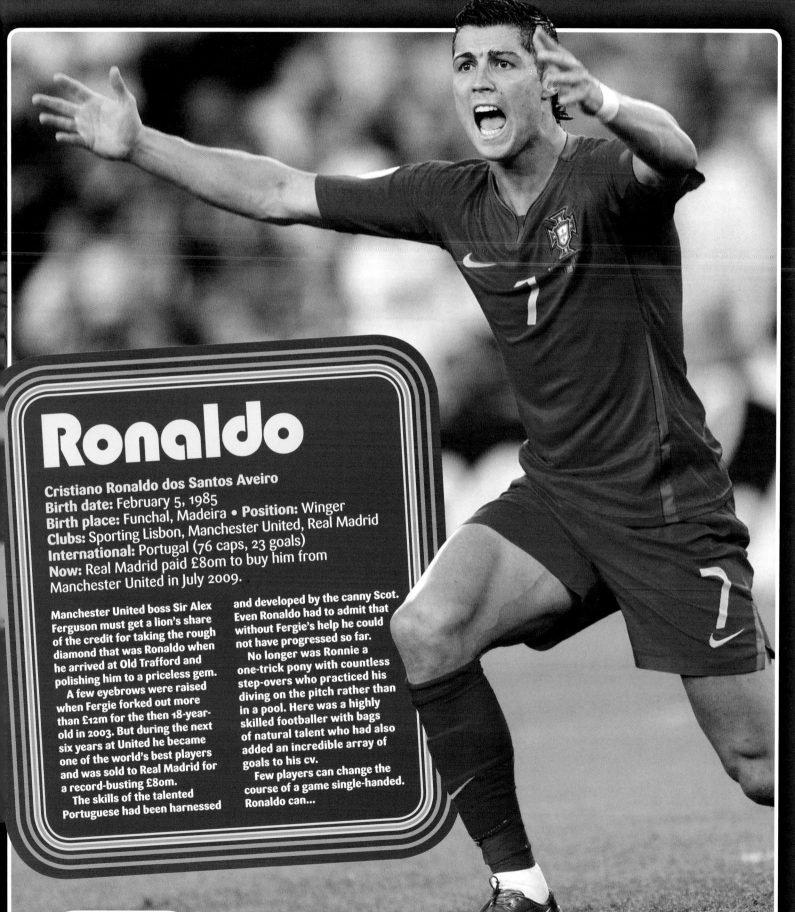

Ronaldo

Cristiano Ronaldo dos Santos Aveiro
Birth date: February 5, 1985
Birth place: Funchal, Madeira • **Position:** Winger
Clubs: Sporting Lisbon, Manchester United, Real Madrid
International: Portugal (76 caps, 23 goals)
Now: Real Madrid paid £80m to buy him from Manchester United in July 2009.

Manchester United boss Sir Alex Ferguson must get a lion's share of the credit for taking the rough diamond that was Ronaldo when he arrived at Old Trafford and polishing him to a priceless gem.

A few eyebrows were raised when Fergie forked out more than £12m for the then 18-year-old in 2003. But during the next six years at United he became one of the world's best players and was sold to Real Madrid for a record-busting £80m.

The skills of the talented Portuguese had been harnessed and developed by the canny Scot. Even Ronaldo had to admit that without Fergie's help he could not have progressed so far.

No longer was Ronnie a one-trick pony with countless step-overs who practiced his diving on the pitch rather than in a pool. Here was a highly skilled footballer with bags of natural talent who had also added an incredible array of goals to his cv.

Few players can change the course of a game single-handed. Ronaldo can...

NOW

Maldini

Paolo Cesare Maldini • **Birth date:** June 26, 1968
Birth place: Milan, Italy • **Position:** Defender
Clubs: AC Milan • **International:** Italy (126 caps, 7 goals)
Now: Retired.

Italy is noted for its defenders – but none of them are quite like the remarkable Paolo Maldini. He spent all 24-plus years of his career with AC Milan, notching just over 900 appearances for the team.

Add to that his 126 caps for Italy in a career that lasted until he was just a month away from his 41st birthday and it's pretty obvious that he was more than just special.

Maldini played at left back or centre half and was perhaps the player more than any other who made a defender's role more appealing to would-be football stars.

Among his many honours were seven Serie A titles, five Champions Leagues and a whole host of other team and individual awards. Most amazing is the record 168 games he played for Milan in the European Cup/Champions League.

THEN

ITALY

Buffon

Gianluigi Buffon • **Birth date:** January 28, 1978
Birth place: Carrara, Italy • **Position:** Keeper
Clubs: Parma, Juventus
International: Italy (102 caps, 0 goals)
Now: Joined Juve in 2001 for a world record fee for a keeper of £32.6m.

The world of football was stunned when Juventus forked out more than £30m for Buffon but now he has picked up the Serie A Goalkeeper of the Year award nine times it doesn't seem quite a ridiculous fee!

Amazingly, at the age of 32 he could still have years left at the top, although there have been suggestions he would like to test himself away from Italy.

He's now played more than 100 games for his country and is widely regarded as the best keeper in the world at the current time. Buffon is an excellent shot-stopper who was Italy's hero at World Cup 2006 when he helped the side to victory.

He's so dedicated that his team-mates complain that they can't even get the ball past him during training!

NOW

35

Raul

Raúl González Blanco • **Birth date:** June 27, 1977 **Birth place:** Madrid • **Position:** Striker • **Clubs:** Real Madrid, Schalke **International:** Spain (102 caps, 44 goals) • **Now:** Still playing

Quite simply, Raul is a goal machine. Although he was with rivals Atletico Madrid as a boy, the striker joined Real Madrid in his teens. He helped them to lift three Champions League titles during 16 glorious years at the Bernabeu before leaving for Schalke before the start of season 2010-11.

Raul has averaged almost a goal every other game for both club and country.

The word legend is often over-used and it's not normally associated with a player still plying his trade. Raul deserves to be an exception to that rule.

His love affair with Europe's top domestic competition is reflected not just by the silverware but by the fact he is the Champions League's record holder for number of goals, number of appearances and the first to reach the 50-goal mark.

THEN

SPAIN

fabregas

Francesc Fabregas Soler • **Birth date:** May 4, 1987
Birth place: Vilassar de Mar, Spain • **Position:** Midfielder
Clubs: Arsenal • **International:** Spain (54 caps, 6 goals)
Now: Constantly linked with a move back to Barcelona, where he was part of their youth system.

He's been with Arsenal since the age of 16 - and seven years on the midfielder has become a massive hit with Gunners fans, creating records in the process.

Named as their captain at the age of 21, Fabregas has been a vital part of Arsene Wenger's side. He has the ability to turn games on his own thanks to his tenacity, great ball skills, amazing passing and knack of scoring superb goals.

Barcelona lost him as a youngster and have always wanted to nab him back. It's been a constant battle between Barca and Arsenal for his services.

Anyone who follows football knows that an Arsenal side without their inspirational skipper is weaker.

The 2008 PFA Young Player of the Year and named in the Premier League Team of the Year for 2007-08 and 2009-10.

NOW

Bergkamp

Dennis Nicolaas Maria Bergkamp • **Birth date:** May 10, 1969 **Birth place:** Amsterdam • **Position:** Forward **Clubs:** Ajax, Inter Milan, Arsenal • **International:** Holland (79 caps, 37 goals) • **Now:** Has been coaching at Ajax.

The words 'Dutch Master' could easily have been coined to describe Dennis Bergkamp. Voted by Arsenal fans as one of their club's best players ever and with a list of achievements that would be the envy of any player.

He inclues the Dutch title, Dutch Cup, European Cup Winners Cup, UEFA Cup, Premier League and FA Cup among his various team awards. Invidually he was three times top scorer in Holland, twice

Dutch Player of the Year, England's Player of the Year, Football Writers' Player of the Year and Arsenal's Player of the Season in 1998.

Playing mostly as a second striker his sublime skills, creativity and goal-scoring abilities were totally amazing.

The only Dutchman to earn a place in the English Football Hall of Fame and Holland's second-top scorer of all time.

THEN

HOLLAND

Van Persie

Robin van Persie • Birth date: August 6, 1983 • Birth place: Rotterdam, Holland • Position: Striker • Clubs: Feyenoord, Arsenal International: Holland (51 games, 19 goals) Now: A first-choice player for Arsenal who was given a long-term contract.

Van Persie has been likened to his fellow countryman and former Arsenal star Bergkamp. And it's not difficult to see why!

He began as a wide left player but he is equally at home playing as a striker. Van Persie provides no little skill to the side and like Bergy, weighs in with both assists and goals.

His goals ratio for Holland rivals that of Bergkamp and with what could be quite a lengthy international career ahead of him van Persie will be looking to get past his countryman's strike rate.

Arsenal have missed their talented star when he has been hit by injuries - no surprise when you know he scored 20 goals for them in 2008-09 and was named the club's Player of the Season.

NOW

Zidane

Zinedine Yazid Zidane • Birth date: June 23, 1972
Birth place: Marseille, France • **Position:** Midfielder
Clubs: Cannes, Bordeaux, Juventus, Real Madrid
International: France (108 caps, 31 goals)
Now: A football advisor with Real Madrid,
who play for their veterans' side.

Zidane's last competitive game was the 2006 World Cup Final in which France lost to Italy and he was sent-off. But before he received his marching orders he was named the Player of the competition - an award he was allowed to keep.

Zidane is not only one of the best players of the last two decades but one of the best players ever. His incredible skills helped France to win both the 1998 World Cup and Euro 2000.

He collected three World Player of the Year awards - only Brazilian Ronaldo can compete with that - and was only the fourth Frenchman ever to reach the 100-cap mark.

His successful time in Italy with Juventus saw him lift two Serie A titles and earn a then record £45.6m move to Real Madrid in 2001.

Among his successes in Spain were a La Liga title and a Champions League.

THEN

FRANCE

Ribéry

Franck Bilal Ribéry • Birth date: April 7, 1983
Birth place: Boulogne-sur-Mer, France • **Position:**
Winger **Clubs:** Boulogne, Ales, Stade Brestois, Metz,
Galatasaray, Mareseille, Bayern Munich
International: France (48 caps, 7 goals)
Now: Signed a new deal with Bayern to 2015 despite
interest from Manchester United and Chelsea.

It took quite a few club moves before Ribery landed at Bayern Munich and was able to seal his reputation as a tricky and skilled left-winger.

The great man Zidane has been full of praise for Ribery who has twice been France's Player of the Year.

Bayern rate the player in the £80m bracket and he is their highest paid player ever. Since his arrival he has helped the side to the German league and cup double in 2008 and 2010 – the first success also leading to Ribery being made Germany's Player of the Year.

Currently regarded as one of the most skilled players in the world but many feel he has yet to reach his peak and show his true colours on a consistent basis.

NOW

PFA AWARD WINNERS

➲ YOUNG PLAYER OF THE YEAR

James Milner

A superb season for the midfielder, who was Villa's stand-out player as they once again threatened to break the top four.

Those performances, coupled with a World Cup where he was one of few England players to emerge with credit, earned him a £26m move to Manchester City.

It was the highest-scoring season of his career, reaching double-figures for the first time.

He signed off with a goal in his final Villa performance (left) on the opening day of this season and will hope to be amongst the goals for his new club.

Having been brought to the club primarily as a winger, Milner was switched to a more central role early on in the campaign and flourished.

He established himself as Villa's key man and made his England debut in what was a superb season for the former Leeds and Newcastle star.

Milner wants to add more silverware to his Young Player of the Year award, declaring his desire to challenge for the Premier League title with Man City.

Having finished as a runner-up twice last year - in the European Championships with England Under-21s and the League Cup with Villa - Milner will be hoping to taste success with City's host of mega-money signings.

➲ MANAGER OF THE YEAR

Harry Redknapp

Finally 'Arry will get to mix it with the big boys. After years of sterling work at some of the country's more unfashionable clubs, Redknapp was given the opportunity to resurrect a sleeping giant in Tottenham, at the start of the 2008–09 season.

Within two seasons he had guided them to the Champions League for the first time in their history.

His just reward for that achievement was to become the first Englishman to win the Premier League Manager of the Year award, ending a sequence of three successive awards for Sir Alex Ferguson.

Redknapp is only the second non-title winning manager to win the award, following George Burley's success in 2001.

Wayne Rooney

Wayne Rooney landed the PFA Player of the Year Award in 2010 - just reward for an amazing season during which he not only turned in some fantastic performances, but also added a glut of goals.

The Manchester United and England striker, who won the Young Player of the Year Award in 2005, admitted that 2010's silverware capped off a memorable campaign.

"It is a great feeling to win the PFA Players' Player of the Year award especially as it is an award that is voted by the players themselves," said Wayne.

"It is something that I am really proud of and I am delighted. Winning the main honour is something you always want to do."

He beat off rival nominations for Arsenal's Cesc Fabregas, Man City's Carlos Tevez and Didier Drogba of Chelsea.

DIVISIONAL TEAMS OF THE YEAR

PREMIER LEAGUE	CHAMPIONSHIP	LEAGUE ONE	LEAGUE TWO
Joe Hart (Birmingham)	Lee Camp (Forest)	Kelvin Davis (Southampton)	Kasper Schmeichel (Notts County)
Branislav Ivanovic (Chelsea)	Chris Gunter (Forest)	Frazer Richardson (Charlton)	John Brayford (Crewe)
Patrice Evra (Man United)	Jose Enrique (Newcastle)	Ian Harte (Carlisle)	Tom Kennedy (Rochdale)
Richard Dunne (Aston Villa)	Fabricio Coloccini (Newcastle)	Patrick Kisnorbo (Leeds)	Craig Dawson (Rochdale)
Thomas Vermaelen (Arsenal)	Ashley Williams (Swansea)	Gary Doherty (Norwich)	Ian Sharps (Rotherham)
James Milner (Aston Villa)	Graham Dorrans (West Brom)	Wes Hoolahan (Norwich)	Ben Davies (Notts County)
Darren Fletcher (Man United)	Peter Whittingham (Cardiff)	Jason Puncheon (Southampton)	Gary Jones (Rochdale)
Cesc Fabregas (Arsenal)	Kevin Nolan (Newcastle)	Robert Snodgrass (Leeds)	Stephen Dawson (Bury)
Antonio Valencia (Man United)	Charlie Adam (Blackpool)	Nicky Bailey (Charlton)	Nicky Law (Rotherham)
Wayne Rooney (Man United)	Andy Carroll (Newcastle)	Rickie Lambert (Southampton)	Lee Hughes (Notts County)
Didier Drogba (Chelsea)	Michael Chopra (Cardiff)	Grant Holt (Norwich)	Adam Le Fondre (Rotherham)

FOREST'S FINEST!

Viv Anderson wasn't bad either for Arsenal and Man United...

Viv Anderson created football history in 1978 when he became the first black player to pull on an England shirt.

And although he last tied his boots as a professional 15 years ago he is still a figure fondly remembered by true football fans.

As a player he also set other significant milestones - two European Cups with Nottingham Forest; Sir Alex Ferguson's first signing at Man United; an MBE and a place in English football's Hall of Fame.

"Not bad for a skinny kid from Nottingham," smiles the former defender, now 53 but who still looks as though he would be fit enough to take to the pitch.

"His resolute professionalism at right-back and bubbly, contagious enthusiasm in the dressing-room were worth a lot more than the £250,000 we paid for Viv."
Sir Alex Ferguson, Man United manager

"Yes some days you look at a game and think 'I wish I could play today' but generally I get up in the morning and I feel stiff so we will leave that out!"

After a distinguished career that produced 30 England caps, and a total of more than 700 appearances for Forest, Arsenal, Man United, Sheffield Wednesday Barnsley and Middlesbrough, Anderson went into management.

He was player-manager at Barnsley for a season before moving to Middlesbrough as assistant to former England skipper Bryan Robson, where he enjoyed two promotions to the Premier League but also suffered relegation, and appearances in both the FA and League Cup Finals.

"I had a couple of opportunities to go back in but it wasn't quite right at the time and I didn't want to find after six months I was out of a job. You have to be careful what you do. If the right thing had come along... but it hasn't and I have plenty to get on with," Anderson told *Shoot*.

During his early playing days Anderson made a massive statement, something that is hard to accept now with the multi-cultural, multi-national Premier League.

"When I first started in the 1970s it was a big thing but look at most clubs now and they have black faces and Asian faces, although maybe not as many Asians as we would like.

"There is a big mix now. We have come a long way but we shouldn't get too complacent, there is still room for improvement," he points out.

So what was it like when he became the first black player to pull on that England shirt?

"At the time it was quite a big thing, especially on the day. I got letters from the Queen, Elton John, famous people. It was a big thing but I was a mere footballer from Nottingham who used to kick people as my job!

"It was just a matter of doing well and focusing on the day so you didn't let anyone down. It was about trying to do well for the team."

Anderson's standing as player

has earned him a place in Britain's Top 100 black sports people of all time, and that's something that brings a smile to his face.

"People ask me about that and I think has someone got it wrong," he says modestly. But at the same time he recognises the honour: "To be first at anything... my achievement in life can never be beaten. I am very proud to have been the first black full England international.

"Every time I get in a cab in London I get recognised and it amazes me as it's 15 years since I last played. I haven't put that much weight on..."

THREE LEGENDS

Viv Anderson was the first black player to pull on an England shirt. He's also played under three legendary managers. He gave *Shoot* an insight into three of the best bosses ever...

SIR ALEX FERGUSON

MANCHESTER UNITED

"I was the first signing made by Fergie. I think it came about in a game Arsneal v Man United at Old Trafford and I tried to kick Norman Whiteside all afternoon.

We'd been on an 18 game unbeaten run and Norman tried to kick everyone who moved on the park, so I tried to give him a little bit back.

Fergie must have thought 'If you can stand up to Norman Whiteside you can stand up to anyone' and he bought me not long after that.

It was a great honour. It was a club I supported as a lad and went there every school holiday from 15-16 but they said I wouldn't be good enough.

I went back to Nottingham and got a job for five weeks. A Forest scout asked me to play for their youth team and they signed me. I went back to United 15 years later for £250,000!

We went pre-season to Hartlepool and the team was Chris Turner, myself, Kevin Moran, Paul McGrath, Arthur Albiston, Gordon Strachan, Bryan Robson, Norman Whiteside, Jesper Olsen, Mark Hughes and a. n. other.

We were 5-0 down at half-time and that's where the hairdryer started. Tea flying everywhere, all over your face and clothes, up to your face and shouting obscenities. We thought what the hell is this? He was a new manager and we didn't know what to expect.

It had the desired effect... we went out second-half and got beat 5-1!"

SIR BOBBY ROBSON

England

To celebrate the 30th anniversary of Forest's European Cup triumphs, Viv Anderson released a no-nonsense autobiography in which he pulls no punches.

The hardback "First Among Equals" is available with Forest, England, Arsenal, Man United and Sheff Wed dustcovers.

Anderson writes of his playing days, personal life and dealing with racialism. There's an insight into many football greats, including George Best, Terry Venables, Bryan Robson, Sir Alex Ferguson and Brian Clough.

BRIAN CLOUGH

Nottingham Forest

"I have millions of stories about Bobby, a fantastic man, a great enthusiast about football and life in general.

But I always remember meeting Shola Ameobi and asking how he was getting on with Bobby, who was always hopeless about names. And he said: 'He is fine, love him'. Does he remember your name? 'No, he calls me Carl Cort'.

Bobby named the team once and got to centre forward and said Bluther No.9. I said 'Who is Bluther?' We left the team meeting and worked out it was Luther Blisset. He was a fantastic manager, sadly missed.

He tried to learn the language in other countries he went to, and he knew a player. He went to any football match you can possibly imagine to pick a player, that was one of his strengths.

He was never the greatest coach to be honest, but he knew a player and knew how to play them. Credit to him he is one of the better English managers we have ever had and no one said a bad word about him."

"He was a one-off. You would never know from one day to the next if you were playing or even if he would say hello. He got the best out of people.

Look at the Forest team - there were no superstars as such, they were workman-like, Bowyer, Robertson, McGiven, Woodcock and others who came through the ranks.

He nurtured us into a side that won two European Cups - I don't think will ever be done again.

It took Arsenal until a few years ago to beat our record of 39 consecutive wins - for a provincial team like Forest to achieve that... well, you have to pinch yourself sometimes.

Sadly he's not with us now but he was unique. I was 17 and we went to Carlisle and he said 'warm up'. Within five minutes I sat back down as I was a sub.

He turned to me and said 'I thought I had told you to warm up'. I said I had but the crowd had been throwing apples, pears and bananas at me. He just said 'well get me a couple of pears and a banana'.

Cloughie was all about what you did on the pitch. After our first European win, Frank Clark, who had come from Newcastle and was 33 or something like that, said it doesn't get much better.

I was 21 or something - he was right, you don't appreciate it at the time but it doesn't get any better. Then we went on to win it again the next year!"

MARIO BALOTELLI

FACT FILE

BIRTHPLACE:	Palermo, Italy
BIRTH DATE:	August 12, 1990
HEIGHT:	1.90m (6ft 3in)
CLUBS:	Lumezzane, Inter, Man City
JOINED MANCHESTER CITY:	2010
TRANSFER FEE:	£24m

DID YOU KNOW?

Balotelli was born in Palermo to Ghanaian immigrants, who put him up for adoption after a succession of life-threatening complications with his intestines, meant that he needed a host of operations and constant care. He was taken in by an Italian family, the Balotellis.

Super Mario is, without doubt, one of the stars of his generation. The 20-year-old starlet has been hyped as the next big thing to come out of Italy for the last two seasons.

After a tumultuous period with Inter, where he was equally frustrating as he was brilliant, Balotelli has left Italy behind for the bright lights of the Premier League.

His £24m move to Manchester City was perfect for both parties. He gets to take centre stage in the club's revolution, while City sign a youngster with the world at his feet.

Balotelli, who made his Italy debut in August, can play anywhere across the front-line and loves to run at opponents.

The fiery youngster boasts an impressive turn of pace and is something of a dead-ball specialist. With his large, powerful frame, Balotelli can also hold the ball up well.

Despite his tender age, Balotelli already has a bulging trophy cabinet - winning three Series A titles, an Italian Cup, the Champions League and the Italian Super Cup.

The striker had various fall-outs with Jose Mourinho during his time in Milan, but was handed his first-team debut by Roberto Mancini during his time with the Nerazzuri, with Balotelli looking to the City boss as something of a father figure.

Likely to be deployed down the right of City's attack, Balotelli could turn out to be one of the most exciting players the Premier League has seen - if he can keep his temper in check.

What they say: Roberto Mancini, Manchester City manager: "He is young and he works hard during training, he doesn't deserve to be considered a 'bad boy'. I consider him a great player that in the future could become fantastic. He is strong, fast and has great skills. It has not been easy for him to leave Italy, but I think that he will be able to help our team."

He says: "It was very important to me that Mancini is the manager here. If he wasn't, I probably wouldn't have come to City. He always showed faith in me when I played for him."

JAVIER HERNANDEZ

News of the Mexico forward's impending move to Manchester broke before the World Cup, and was something of a shock – United had agreed to shell out approximately £10m (albeit heavily incentive based) on a virtual unknown.

Sir Alex Ferguson's surprise signing made total sense following the player's excellent World Cup displays, bagging goals against big guns France and Argentina.

Suddenly, 'Chicharito' was the name on every United fan's lips – from being an unknown just two months earlier, the young attacker had to contend with a weight of expectation when he joined up with his new side's pre-season camp.

He made an instant impact for United, bagging a goal in his first appearance of their America tour, using his pace to break through and his finishing to calmly lob the keeper.

He repeated the trick in his first full game for United, notching in the Community Shield victory against Chelsea. Though this time his finish was less stylish, scuffing his shot in off his face!

The first Mexican to play for United, his goal-scoring record is terrific – at the time of his arrival at Old Trafford the 22-year-old had bagged ten goals in just 17 appearances for Mexico.

He was also top scorer of the Mexican league last season, scoring 21 goals in 28 games.

Exceedingly quick – the fastest player at the World Cup according to FIFA – two-footed and a deadly finisher, he should fit in well at Old Trafford.

FACT FILE

BIRTH PLACE:	Guadalajara, Mexico
BIRTH DATE:	June 1, 1988
HEIGHT:	1.75m (5ft 9in)
CLUBS:	Guadalajara, Manchester United
JOINED MANCHESTER UNITED:	2010
TRANSFER FEE:	Undisclosed

DID YOU KNOW?

Hernandez's nickname 'Chichartio' (meaning 'little pea') was given to him as his father, also a professional footballer, was known as 'Chicharo' ('pea') because of his vivid green eyes.

What they say: Sir Alex Ferguson, Man United manager: "Chicharito has done really well. The players have all remarked how good he is and what a great finisher he is – I think there are similarities between him and Ole Gunnar Solskjaer. I think he has a great future with us."

He says: "I got goose-bumps when I realised I would be joining Manchester United. These are the things you dream about. I'm just full of gratitude to everyone who helped me accomplish this. Suddenly I'm going to be playing with the players I know from PlayStation and television. I'm living in a dream."

DIDIER DROGBA

ⓘ FACT FILE

BIRTH PLACE:	Abidjan, Ivory Coast
BIRTH DATE:	March 11, 1978
HEIGHT:	1.88m (6ft 2in)
CLUBS:	Le Mans, Guingamp, Marseille, Chelsea
JOINED CHELSEA:	2004
TRANSFER FEE:	£24m

DID YOU KNOW?

He is the Ivory Coast's all-time record scorer.

The burly Ivorian forward has established himself as one of the world's best, having completed a dramatic transformation from France's lower leagues to the pinnacle of European football.

Possessor of incredible upper body strength, a unique ability to create space for himself and a pile-driver of a shot, Drogba has captured the imagination of fans worldwide.

The striker has become an icon not only to his home country, but his home continent of Africa – becoming synonymous with African football. It is a role he takes seriously and has often intervened in political situations, using football as a vehicle for change.

A powerhouse of a player, Drogba is criticised at times for his on-field theatrics, but pressed on his habit to dive, simply said it is a part of football.

Drogba has won everything in the English game during his time with Chelsea, except the Champions League. In Chelsea's sole final appearance, he was dismissed for violent conduct in extra-time.

But it is his tenacious, volatile playing style that makes him such a threat. Brilliantly skilful, clinical and outrageously talented, Drogba can, at times, be frustrating. He can be absent from games, doing little more than walking around moaning. Then, in a flash of class, he can take the game by the horns and seal victory.

WHAT THEY SAY: Chelsea boss Carlo Ancelotti: "Drogba is a very important player for us. I think he's irreplaceable as no other striker in the world can do the same job. I've spoken with him and know very well what he wants. I believe in Drogba and told him this."

HE SAYS: "In my third season here I scored 20 goals in the league, in this one [2009–10] I scored 29 – it's amazing. I really feel season after season I'm getting better. I always keep working. I'm not Messi or Cristiano Ronaldo but I have my own qualities so I work on them and always try to improve my weak points."

WAYNE ROONEY

Dubbed the 'White Pele', Wayne Rooney is probably the most talented English player to emerge for decades.

Who could forget the moment he announced himself to the world? Spectacularly ending Arsenal's dominant winning streak by powering a blistering strike beyond David Seaman for Everton, instantly captured the imagination of the entire nation.

His rise was swift, quickly becoming the focal point of the England team despite his tender years. His exploits at Euro 2004 confirmed him as one of the world's brightest prospects and his mega-money move to Manchester United was no surprise.

His Old Trafford debut was even more spectacular than his Everton equivalent – participating in his first Champions League tie he grabbed a stunning hat-trick against Fenerbahce.

Since then his talent has been nurtured carefully under the watchful gaze of Sir Alex Ferguson and Rooney has now claimed every major honour available at club level – the FA Cup the only exception, having lost on both of his final appearances.

Rooney has the world at his feet, but stills plays as if he were having a kick-about on the streets.

Fiery, passionate and gifted, Rooney is the player every Englishman admires most.

What they say: Sir Alex Ferguson, Man United boss: "Giving him the direct role has given him an appetite to be in the box all the time. He still has moments when he goes into other areas of the pitch but he is choosing those moments more maturely. The main reason he is scoring the goals is because he is in the right place at the right time."

He says: "The manager said to me I needed to score more headers. But I was playing out wide a lot back then. He said he wanted me in the box more and that I had drifted wide too much. I had to try to control my energy, stay in the box, so when the chances came I had the energy to take them."

ⓘ FACT FILE

BIRTH PLACE:	Croxteth,Liverpool.
BIRTH DATE:	October 24, 1986
HEIGHT:	1.78m (5ft 10 in)
CLUBS:	Everton, Man United
JOINED MAN UNITED:	2004
TRANSFER FEE:	£25.6m

DID YOU KNOW?

Rooney became England's youngest player when he made his debut against Australia in 2003, and the youngest to score for the country when he notched in Euro 2004. Both records have since been broken.

PETER CROUCH

ⓘ FACT FILE

BIRTH PLACE:	Macclesfield, Cheshire
BIRTH DATE:	January 30, 1981
HEIGHT:	2m (6ft 7in)
CLUBS:	QPR, Portsmouth, Aston Villa, Southampton, Liverpool, Tottenham
JOINED TOTTENHAM:	2009
TRANSFER FEE:	£10m

DID YOU KNOW?

Crouch started his career at Tottenham, joining as a schoolboy in 1991 before leaving in 2000 having never played for Spurs.

Initially mocked for his incredible height, Peter Crouch has since established himself as a worthy top-flight player, and dispelled criticisms that were based on little more than stereotype.

Unlike the popular opinion that tall players are useless with their feet, Crouch is a cultured player with the technique of a creative midfielder. His height obviously makes him a threat in the air, while his finishing completes his role as 'impact player'.

Many managers would prefer to use him from the bench as a game changer. To be trusted as 'match-winner' is testament to Crouch's true ability and though he will never be the most fashionable of forwards or as clinical as some of his contemporaries, the striker offers an excellent all-round package.

This has been demonstrated by his superb goal-scoring record with England and, despite being third-choice forward at club level, he was included in England's World Cup squad last summer.

What they say: Spurs boss Harry Redknapp: "He leads the line well and holds the ball up. He gives you something different when games are tight. You can play long balls to him, he will win headers and let other players get around the second ball and open packed defences."

He says: "Harry has got the best out of me. I also played for him at Portsmouth and for a short spell at Southampton. Whenever I've played for him, I've always played well. He does get the best out of footballers."

THIERRY HENRY

Nice guy Thierry Henry, practically adopted by England after the country was endeared to his amiable charm during his Arsenal days, become an overnight villain after his 'hand of frog' goal against the Republic of Ireland.

This indiscretion cannot mask the impact Henry had on English football. He is, without doubt, one of the best players to have graced the Premier League and one of the greatest to have represented Arsenal.

His exploits helped transform the Gunners into Champions, the Incredibles who went a whole season unbeaten, and even Champions League finalists.

Henry's place in Arsenal history is already assured, he is the club's leading all time goal-scorer, and the successes he has enjoyed since joining Barcelona have justified his decision to leave London.

In just three seasons at the Camp Nou, Henry matched the seven pieces of silverware he lifted during his eight-year spell with Arsenal – including winning the Champions League for the first time.

He has also won the World Cup, European Championships and ConfederationsCup with France and the French top-flight with Monaco early in his career.

ℹ FACT FILE

BIRTH PLACE:	Essonne, France
BIRTH DATE:	August 17, 1977
HEIGHT:	1.89m (6ft 2in)
CLUBS:	Monaco, Juventus, Arsenal, Barcelona, New York Red Bulls
JOINED BARCELONA:	2007
TRANSFER FEE:	£20m

DID YOU KNOW?

Henry was top scorer in his first season at Barcelona. In his second season, he was a part of the most prolific strikeforce in Spanish history — Henry, Messi and Eto'o breaking the record set by legendary trio Puskas, Di Stefano and del Sol.

What they say:
Former Arsenal and France team-mate Patrick Vieira: "Henry's got the talent, he's got the experience and Thierry is one of the players who can win games by himself."

He Says: "People say my
game has changed since and I say that it's good that it changed, otherwise it would show a lack of intelligence."

CARLOS TEVEZ

Carlos Tevez loves football and works hard to be successful.

His hard-work and combative style has endeared him to fans of every club he has represented, while his goal-scoring hasn't gone unnoticed either.

He announced himself in England with West Ham, scoring the goals that preserved the Hammers' top-flight status. Though his time at Upton Park was brief, he will always be guaranteed a warm reception for almost single-handedly keeping the Hammers up.

At Manchester United, his quality was questioned when placed alongside the likes of Cristiano Ronaldo, Wayne Rooney and Dimitar Berbatov, but his intense work ethic and never-say-die attitude made him a hero.

When he began to feel unwanted at Old Trafford, as the club desperately haggled for a lower transfer fee, Tevez found the welcoming home of Man City, much to the annoyance of his former employers.

He plundered a host of goals for the Eastlands outfit, including a stand-out performance against United in the League Cup semi-final. Though his side were defeated, he reminded the United fans exactly what they were missing.

What they say: Diego Maradona, Argentina coach, once described Tevez as: "The Argentine prophet for the 21st Century."

He says: "I love the Manchester derby. It is special, different. There is an argument going on in my head about why I feel so strongly about it. It is nothing to do with the spotlight being on me, I did not transfer from United to City for the controversy."

ROBBIE KEANE

What they say:

Harry Redknapp, Spurs boss: "I don't see us loaning Robbie out again. We paid a lot of money for him, so it's not something I see happening. I certainly would not want it to be happening."

He says: "For me, it is just about playing games. As a player, you lose confidence sometimes. It is important you try to get that back as soon as possible."

Robbie Keane is a player of immense talent. From his move to Italian giants Inter Milan to his ill-fated six-month spell at Liverpool, his career points to various 'might have beens'.

Until his move to Liverpool in 2008, Keane was regarded as possibly the best player outside of the 'Big Four'. He even fired Tottenham to League Cup success.

His exploits earned him a move to Liverpool, the shot at the big time that he deserved, but it was to end in disaster.

Kop boss Rafa Benitez never seemed to fancy him and later revealed Keane wasn't the player he had wanted to sign. Benitez eventually shipped Keane back to Tottenham.

This dented the striker's confidence and Keane found himself falling down the pecking order at White Hart Lane.

A loan move to Celtic gave him regular first-team football and reinvigorated the hitman.

FACT FILE

BIRTH PLACE:	Dublin, Ireland
BIRTH DATE:	July 8, 1980
HEIGHT:	1.75m (5ft 9in)
CLUBS:	Wolves, Coventry, Inter Milan, Leeds, Tottenham, Liverpool, Celtic (loan)
JOINED TOTTENHAM:	2002 and 2009.
TRANSFER FEE:	£12m

DID YOU KNOW?

Keane was part of the Ireland Under-18 team that won the European Championships in 1998.

FERNANDO TORRES

FACT FILE

BIRTH PLACE:	Fuenlabrada, Spain.
BIRTH DATE:	March 20, 1984
HEIGHT:	1.85m (6ft 1in)
PREVIOUS CLUBS:	Atletico Madrid
JOINED LIVERPOOL:	2007
TRANSFER FEE:	£24m

DID YOU KNOW?

While playing for Atletico, Torres accidentally dropped his captain's armband revealing a personally inscribed message which read "You'll never walk alone" – Liverpool's slogan. This endeared him to the Anfield faithful before his arrival at the club.

The accolade of 'best striker in the world' is difficult to assign. There are many contenders.

But few would argue with Fernando Torres being handed the accolade.

He emerged as a bright young talent with hometown club Atletico Madrid, but showed a ruthless streak in leaving the club he loved in pursuit of success.

His chosen destination was Anfield, with some suggesting he was a Liverpool fan. He went on to become Rafa Benitez's biggest success story.

Already a talented forward upon arrival in England, Benitez helped develop the frontman into one of the world's elite.

Though the success he craved didn't arrive, world-wide recognition did. The Spaniard now stands as one of the most feared attackers in the world.

His elegant playing style, his dribbling and finishing, combined with his goal-scoring habit, make him a player to admire.

What they say: Steven Gerrard, Anfield team-mate: "When you have players like Torres on the team you know there's always a chance. Everyone knows when he's on form he's the best in the world."

He says: "People had told me about all about Anfield, about the atmosphere, about You'll Never Walk Alone. But I never really knew what it was like until I had the chance to live it. It was just amazing."

ROBIN VAN PERSIE

What they say: Arsene Wenger, Arsenal manager: "He had an 'attitude' but what saves people, always, is a love for football and an intelligence. Robin is at an age where a football player becomes really efficient, mature, and wants to win things. That is why I believe he can be the best passer in the league and he can be the best goal-scorer in the league."

He says: "When I look at a football pitch I see it as my canvas. I see solutions, possibilities, the space to express myself. I am always looking for ways to be creative, to gain an edge. I wasn't artistic in drawing or painting but I think I am in sport. It's a challenge that excites me."

Brought up in a household of art lovers, it should be no surprise that Van Persie's game is so artistic.

As a youngster, his parents tried to teach him the ways of art, but he admitted that it just didn't click. "My parents could look at a tree and see something marvellous, whereas I'd look at it and see just a tree."

Arsenal boss Arsene Wenger has compared van Persie to a combination of Arsenal greats - Thierry Henry and Denis Bergkamp.

He can finish, has the ability to pick out intricate passes and move and the raw talent necessary to turn a game on its head.

The Dutch forward offers an option that is incomparable throughout Europe. His style is exceptional.

Neither gifted with tremendous pace, nor a sizeable frame, van Persie is neither target man or second striker. And yet he can fill both roles tremendously.

His strength is deceptive and, while he is certainly no slouch, he doesn't need to rely on pace like less technically gifted players.

ⓘ FACT FILE

BIRTH PLACE:	Rotterdam, Holland
BIRTH DATE:	August 6, 1983
HEIGHT:	1.82m (6ft)
CLUBS:	Feyenoord, Arsenal
JOINED ARSENAL:	2004
TRANSFER FEE:	£2.75m

DID YOU KNOW?

Van Persie left SBV Excelsior, whom he had joined as a four-year-old, after falling out with the club aged just 16. He went to Feyenoord but fell out with manager Bert van Marwijk on various occasions — prompting his move to Arsenal on the cheap.

CARLTON COLE

(i) FACT FILE

BIRTH PLACE:	Croydon, London
BIRTH DATE:	November 12, 1983
HEIGHT:	1.91m (6ft 3in)
CLUBS:	Chelsea, Wolves (loan), Charlton (loan), Aston Villa (loan), West Ham
JOINED WEST HAM:	2006
TRANSFER FEE:	Undisclosed

DID YOU KNOW?

Cole, of Nigerian and Sierra Leon descent, decided early on that it was his intention to play for England. However, in 2008, Cole accepted a call up for the Nigeria team, only to be told he was too old to switch national teams. Just four months later he made his England debut.

After an up and down start to his career, where it appeared as if he'd never settle into a regular goal-scoring pattern no matter where he went, Cole has found himself a home with West Ham.

A Chelsea youngster, Cole had loan spells with Wolves, Charlton and Aston Villa before eventually joining the Hammers in 2006, where he has established himself as Premier League quality.

That ability was apparent early on, as then Chelsea boss Claudio Ranieri raved about Cole in 2002.

"I've never coached a young player like Carlton," the Italian said. "He's fantastic even though he hasn't really started his career yet. He has a very long contract, and, in my opinion, a very big future at Chelsea."

With such a glowing reference, it was little wonder that Cole's inconsistency provoked such frustration.

Having signed for West Ham in 2006, he again initially struggled to make an impact. He was predominantly a substitute during his first season at Upton Park, before gradually growing into the jersey the following year.

The 2008-09 season proved a turning point in his career – reaching double figures for the first time, establishing himself as first-choice for the Hammers, earning a five-year deal and making his England debut. He followed that last season by again top-scoring for the Clarets, and will start this campaign as undoubted first-choice at the Boelyn Ground – with a host of big clubs watching on enviously.

What they say: Former West Ham manager Gianfranco Zola: "More than any other player, he reminds me of Mark Hughes, especially when he's holding the ball up. He's also very fast. All he has to improve is his finishing, which is maybe not as good as his control of the ball, but he's on the way, he's working hard and I'm sure he'll fill that gap."

He says: "I've never been happier than where I am. It'd take an awful lot for me to move away. I see my future here at Upton Park, nowhere else. I'll never forget West Ham were the club who gave me my big break in the Premier League. I want to repay that faith they had in me."

DAVID SILVA

Internationally, jet-heeled winger David Silva has practically won it all. The 2004 Under-19 European Championships, the 2008 senior European Championships, the 2010 World Cup.

He was also part of the Spain team that finished third in the 2009 Confederations Cup.

Domestically, with the exception of the 2007 Copa del Ray, those successes weren't mirrored.

At Valencia he and David Villa were big fish in a small pond. The key duo carried their side to the Champions League, but each craved further success.

It was no coincidence that both sought pastures new in summer 2010. Silva's £25m arrival at Manchester City may have caught the headlines for the transfer fee involved, but it was widely overlooked that the club had landed a world-class player.

A winger like the Ryan Giggs of old, Silva is electric in possession, darting down the left flank to deadly effect.

Though he will be displacing a City favourite in Craig Bellamy, Silva's undoubted ability will surely win over the fans.

A creative force that can also be deployed in the traditional number ten role – or 'playmaker' in the age of limitless squad numbers – Silva will slot nicely into the left-hand side of City's attack.

(i) FACT FILE

BIRTH PLACE:	Arguineguin, Spain
BIRTH DATE:	January 8, 1986
HEIGHT:	1.70m (5ft 7in)
CLUBS:	Valencia, Eibar (loan), Celta Vigo (loan), Manchester City
JOINED MANCHESTER CITY:	2010
TRANSFER FEE:	£25m

DID YOU KNOW?

Silva progressed through the international ranks at a phenomenal pace — going from representing Spain at the Under–17 level to the full side in less than three years. Even more remarkable, he played for the Under–19s, Under–20s and Under–21s in that brief period!

What they say: Roberto Mancini, Man City manager: "I think that David Silva is one of the best midfielders in Europe, and I hope he will be a very important player for Manchester City. I am so pleased he has come to us. I think he can make a big, big impact. In signing David, we are showing the world that we are bringing the best players here and that we hope to compete to win the Premier League."

He Says: "The time is right for me to seek a new challenge, and I am thrilled about playing in England with Manchester City. I believe the Premier League is one of the best competitions in the world and I want to bring success to City and win trophies for them."

MY FAVOURITE PLAYER

CURRENT STARS NOMINATE THE TOP FOOTBALLERS WHOSE SILKY SKILLS THEY ADMIRE MOS[T]

LIONEL MESSI **ARGENTINA**

NOMINATED BY: John Terry, Chelsea

"He is so good - incredible and unplayable at times. If he comes inside at any time you need two men to double up on him. You can't get near him in a one on one. He is a special talent, especially when he is performing at the Nou Camp."

STEVEN GERRARD **ENGLAND**

NOMINATED BY: Lucas, Liverpool

"There are similarities between Stevie and Kaka but Stevie makes more of a contribution all over the pitch. He's more complete because he can attack as well as defend. He is so good he could probably play anywhere."

FERNANDO TORRES SPAIN

NOMINATED BY: Darren Bent, Sunderland

"He is one of the best strikers in the world. He's brilliant and when he is playing at his best he is unstoppable. If I can be up there with him in the scoring charts I will be delighted."

JAMES MILNER ENGLAND

NOMINATED BY:
John Carew, Aston Villa

"He is strong mentally and James has a great football head as well as the skills. He still chases the ball to the corner flag in the final minute when most people's legs have gone, he is amazing."

RYAN GIGGS WALES

NOMINATED BY: Phil Neville, Everton

I think he is the greatest player ever to play for Man United. I know United have had some great players but he's won everything, he's broken almost every record, so he stands alone now as probably one of the greatest players who has ever lived."

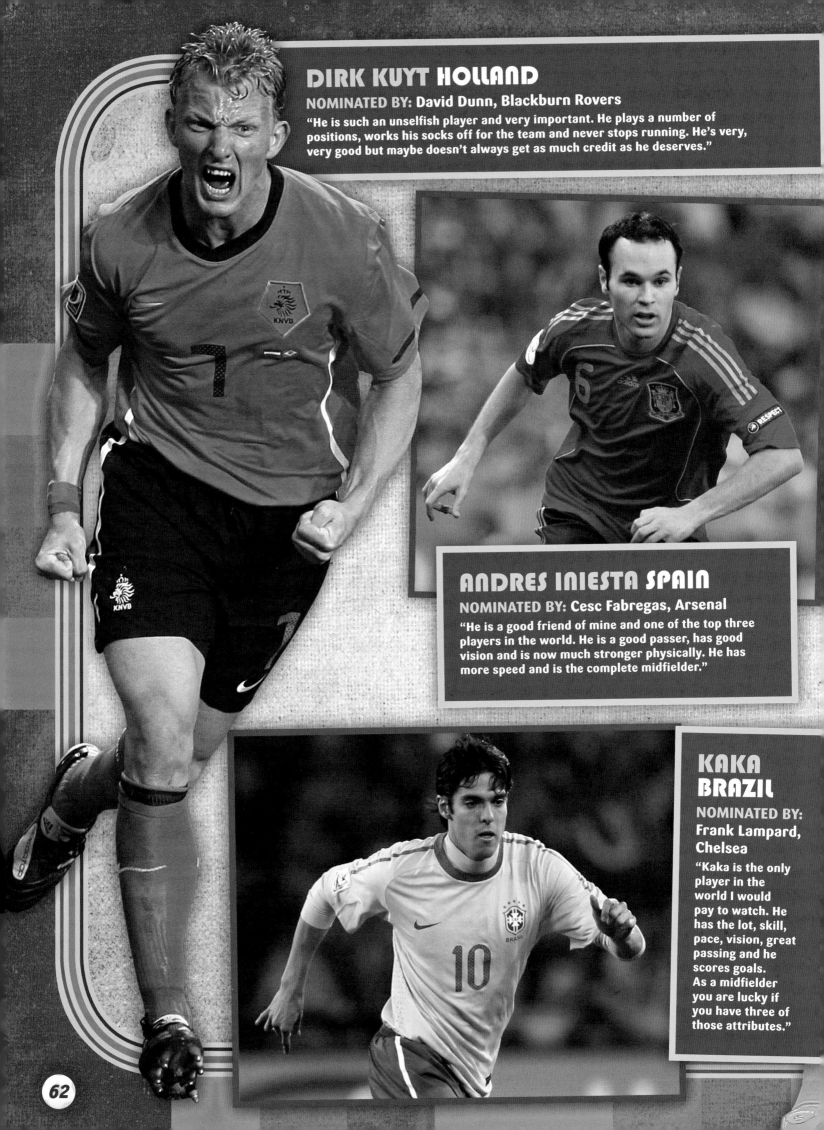

DIRK KUYT HOLLAND

NOMINATED BY: David Dunn, Blackburn Rovers

"He is such an unselfish player and very important. He plays a number of positions, works his socks off for the team and never stops running. He's very, very good but maybe doesn't always get as much credit as he deserves."

ANDRES INIESTA SPAIN

NOMINATED BY: Cesc Fabregas, Arsenal

"He is a good friend of mine and one of the top three players in the world. He is a good passer, has good vision and is now much stronger physically. He has more speed and is the complete midfielder."

KAKA BRAZIL

NOMINATED BY: Frank Lampard, Chelsea

"Kaka is the only player in the world I would pay to watch. He has the lot, skill, pace, vision, great passing and he scores goals. As a midfielder you are lucky if you have three of those attributes."

CRISTIANO RONALDO PORTUGAL

NOMINATED BY: Thierry Henry, France

"Ronaldo is better than Messi. The greatness of a player is measured by the titles he has helped a team win. They are different and both have extraordinary technique but Ronaldo has scored more goals. Right now he is the best."

EMMANUEL ADEBAYOR TOGO

NOMINATED BY: Michael Dawson, Tottenham

"He is simply a good player. He is a big strong lad who can hold the ball up. He is going to fight and when you walk off that pitch you know you have been in a battle."

CLASSIC IMAGE

GAZZA'S TEARS

The 1990 World Cup semi-final was just a bit too much for Paul Gascoigne. The Geordie genius was on the verge of appearing in the final but a booking in the game against Germany meant he would miss the biggest game of his career if the Three Lions progressed. He needn't have worried. Sir Bobby Robson's side failed in a penalty shoot-out but before that happened Gazza had watered the pitch with his tears and won over the hearts of a nation.

Summer Transfer Update

RECESSION? WHAT RECESSION? Summer 2010 transfer activity was as vibrant as ever. With Manchester City's huge spending acting as a catalyst and the World Cup a very prominent showcase, some of the globe's hottest talents were on the move. We round the biggest movers and shakers across Europe. ➲

MOURINHO'S MADRID

Special One looks to reign in Spain

It was inevitable, wasn't it? Jose Mourinho, the world's highest rated manager, was always going to be destined to take the helm of Real Madrid, the stand-out team in football history.

After guiding Inter Milan to a superb treble, which included his second Champions League crown, the Portuguese coach swapped Milan for Madrid.

His coaching pedigree is unrivalled: winning league and cup Doubles in the top tier of three different countries - Portugal with Porto, England with Chelsea and Italy with Inter.

He was just the third manager of all time to win the European Cup with two different teams (Porto and Inter), following Ernst Happel and Ottmar Hitzfeld.

Since 2002, his arrival at Porto, Mourinho has not had a single trophy-less season, while last season's Treble with Inter was the second of his career - repeating the feat he achieved with Porto in 2003.

The only other manager to win trebles with two different clubs? Sir Alex Ferguson! Mourinho is truly up there with the world's elite.

He will look to use the Bernebeu as a home fortress, something he has done at each of his previous three clubs.

Remarkably, the self-proclaimed 'Special One' could boast an unbeaten league home record throughout his time at Porto, Chelsea and Inter; an incredible 136-game streak

Maintaining that formidable record will be key in his attempts to wrestle the league title away from arch-rivals Barcelona, where he once served as assistant manager to Sir Bobby Robson.

 FACT FILE

BIRTH PLACE:	Setubal, Portugal
BIRTH DATE:	January 26, 1973
POSITION:	Manager
HEIGHT:	1.79m (5ft 10in)
CLUBS (PLAYING CAREER):	Rio Ave,
	Belenenses,
	Sesimbra,
	Comercio e Industria
CLUBS (MANAGERIAL CAREER):	
	Benfica,
	Uniao de Leiria, Porto,
	Chelsea, Inter,
	Real Madrid

DID YOU KNOW?

Mourinho followed his father, also called Jose but referred to as Felix, into football. Felix Mourinho was a professional goalkeeper, earning a solitary Potugal cap, before going into coaching and management. Like father, like son!

RECLAIMING THEIR CROWN...
The players he has brought in to rule La Liga

Mesut Özil

ℹ FACT FILE

BIRTH PLACE:	Gelsenkirchen, Germany
BIRTH DATE:	October 15, 1988
POSITION:	Attacking midfielder
HEIGHT:	1.82m (6ft 0in)
CLUBS:	Rot-Weiss Essen, Schalke, Werder Bremen, Real Madrid

DID YOU KNOW?

Born of Turkish descent, Ozil is deeply religious and recites verses from the Qur'an before each game. He was part of Schalke's first-team squad at the tender age of 16!

Özil first came to prominence in a stunning Germany victory over England, inspiring his nation's Under-21 side to a 4-0 drubbing of England's equivalent during the European Championships final.

Sound familiar? Two days short of exactly a year later, he was terrorising England's senior side as he illuminated the 2010 World Cup with his sparkling performances.

As part of an unfancied Germany side that finished third in South Africa, Özil was suddenly the hottest property in world football. Unfortunately for his club, Werder Bremen, he only had one season remaining on his contract.

A player that surely otherwise would've commanded a fee in excess of £30m given his sublime performances over the summer, was available for less than half that price.

Real will look to the mercurial talent to step into the shoes of out-going Guti, providing a creative force to unlock defences for the wealth of attacking options around him.

Ricardo Carvalho

ℹ FACT FILE

BIRTH PLACE:	Amarante, Portugal
BIRTH DATE:	May 18, 1978
POSITION:	Centre back
HEIGHT:	1.83m (6ft 0in)
CLUBS:	Porto, Leca (loan), Vitoria de Setubal (loan), Alverca (loan), Chelsea, Real Madrid

DID YOU KNOW?

Carvalho could've joined Real Madrid six years ago when he left Porto, only to decide to follow manager Jose Mourinho to newly-rich Chelsea. This is the third time Carvalho will have played under Mourinho's tutelage.

Widely regarded as the reason for Chelsea's defensive strength under Mourinho, Carvalho was always going to be on the radar of his former coach and good friend.

Probably the most complete defender in world football, Carvalho has made his intentions clear from the beginning - saying that he wants to win the Champions League with Madrid, the one trophy that eluded him at Chelsea.

Part of the Portugal side that reached the 2004 European Championships final, the classy centre back will add steel to a Real Madrid backline that has been notoriously shaky in the past.

Angel di Maria

Argentina winger di Maria rose to prominence in Europe with Benfica and was widely linked with moves to the continent's elite throughout last season. An impressive World Cup confirmed Madrid's interest and a deal worth up to £30m.

Sergio Canales

One of the most exciting Spanish prospects for a long time, Canales exploded into the Racing Santander first-team last season, earning rave reviews across Europe. The attacking midfielder will have plenty of competition for places, but the teenager has plenty of time to breakthrough.

Sami Khedira

Another member of Germany's impressive World Cup squad, Khedira provided the midfield anchor that allowed Özil space to roam. Despite an already crowded engine room at Madrid, the former Stuttgart man is expected to establish himself this season.

HEY BIG SPENDER

City's record outlay shocks the continent

Since arriving in Manchester during August 2008, the Abu Dhabi United Group has been full of surprises.

Taking control of City, a club that had been in the third tier of English football in the not-so-distant past, on the day the summer transfer window closed, the new board wasted no time in making their mark - shelling out a British record £32.5m for Real Madrid's Robinho.

In summer 2009 the club spent over £100m to build on the initial signings, but even that pales in comparison to the activity seen during the 2010 close-season.

Roberto Mancini has overseen the arrivals of some of the biggest names in world football, for a combined fee of over £150m.

They plucked World Cup winner David Silva from Valencia, Champions League winner Mario Balotelli from Inter and Spanish champion Yaya Toure from Barcelona as the Eastlands club set about trying to achieve their dream of Champions League qualification.

Having finished fifth in season 2009-10, just three points adrift of the coveted top four, the only way is up for City!

Jerome Boateng

ⓘ FACT FILE

BIRTH PLACE:	Berlin, Germany
BIRTH DATE:	September 3, 1988
POSITION:	Full back, centre back
HEIGHT:	1.92m (6ft 4in)
CLUBS:	Hertha Berlin, Hamburg, Man City
INTERNATIONAL:	Germany

DID YOU KNOW?

Born to a German mother and Ghanaian father, Boateng was eligible for either nation. Unlike half-brother Kevin-Prince, though, Boateng elected to play for Germany. The pair fell out over Kevin-Prince's tackle on Michael Ballack in last season's 2010 FA Cup final, ruling the German skipper out of the World Cup.

A rock solid defender capable of playing virtually anywhere along the backline, Boateng's arrival may not be the highest profile, but it could certainly have the biggest effect.

A team that looked good going forward last season, but vulnerable at the back, Boateng will add assurance and composure to City's defence.

Part of the Hamburg side that reached successive Europa League semi finals, Boateng excelled at the 2010 World Cup (what Germany player didn't?) and his £10.4m transfer already looks a snip.

Yaya Toure

ⓘ FACT FILE

BIRTH PLACE:	Sekoura Bouake, Ivory Coast
BIRTH DATE:	May 13, 1983
POSITION:	Holding midfielder
HEIGHT:	1.91m (6ft 3in)
CLUBS:	Mimosas, Beveren, Metalurh Donetsk, Olympiacos, Monaco, Barcelona, Man City
INTERNATIONAL:	Ivory Coast

DID YOU KNOW?

The deal to reunite Yaya with his brother Kolo has caught the imagination of the fans – a Champions League winner and part of the Barcelona side that won an unprecedented sextuple, he's a signing of the highest calibre. His huge wage – reportedly an astronomical £200,000 a week! – has also been well documented.

A player who could probably walk into the starting line-up of any side in the world. Except Barcelona's.

Frustrated at being usurped by Sergio Busquets at the Nou Camp, Toure sought a move to the Premier League and, specifically, the challenge of establishing Manchester City as a European powerhouse.

A title-winner already in Ivory Coast, Greece and Spain, Toure is looking to lift his fourth different national title with City.

A player who will offer a protective shield in front of Man City's defence, Toure has an engine that allows him to bomb forward too, when necessary.

Probably the signing that has helped more than any other to change City's title aspirations from 'fantastical' to 'very possible'.

Aleksandar Kolarov

ⓘ FACT FILE

BIRTH PLACE:	Belgrade, Serbia
BIRTH DATE:	November 10, 1985
POSITION:	Left back
HEIGHT:	1.87m (6ft 1in)
CLUBS:	Cukaricki Stankm, OFK Beograd, Lazio, Man City
INTERNATIONAL:	Serbia

DID YOU KNOW?

Kolarov joined Lazio for just £750,000 in the summer of 2007, meaning that this summer's £16m switch made the Rome club more than 2000% profit!

A player that has gone from footballing obscurity to worldwide headlines in the space of just three years.

At the end of the 2007 season, Kolarov was plying his trade in the top tier of Serbian football. Now, three years on, he will form an essential part of one of the continent's most heavily scrutinised teams.

An attacking full back, Kolarov has naturally earned comparisons to Brazil great Roberto Carlos.

Known for his runs down the left flank and the power with which he shoots, the comparison isn't unfair.

Kolarov, though, has a bigger frame and is therefore stronger in the challenge and more dangerous from set-pieces.

Summer Transfer Update!

PREMIER LEAGUE NEW BOYS

Some of the lesser-known arrivals

Summer 2010 saw a host of new faces in the Premier League, which we're sure you know all about (if not, you should have been checking out www.shoot.co.uk). We thought we'd give you a more in-depth introduction to three of the division's lesser known recruits...

Nikola Zigic

ℹ FACT FILE

BIRTH PLACE:	Backa Topola, Serbia
BIRTH DATE:	September 25, 1980
POSITION:	Striker
HEIGHT:	2.02m (6ft 7_in)
CLUBS:	Backa Topola, Mornar Bar, Kolubara Lazarevac, Spartak Subotica, Red Star, Racing Santander, Valencia, Birmingham

DID YOU KNOW?

Zigic will be the Premier League's tallest player, ousting former incumbent Peter Crouch by just half an inch! Still, we bet Zigic can't do the robot...

After Birmingham reached the lofty heights of the Premier League's top half last season, Alex McLeish turned to giant striker Zigic to help his side acclimitise!

A £6m recruit from Valencia, his signing is seen as something of a snip - as he had arrived at the Mestalla for £20m just three years earlier.

Obviously a threat in the air, Zigic is handy with his feet, too - making him a real threat in front of goal.

Given Brum's meagre goalscoring record last term (they averaged just a goal a game), the onus will be on the Serbia hitman to fire the Blues up the table.

Sandro

The £14m signing arrived late at White Hart Lane, but he had a very good excuse - he was busy helping former club Internacional win the Copa Libertadores, the South American Champions League.

Harry Redknapp will hope the Brazil midfielder can use the momentum from that victory to help introduce a winning culture at Spurs.

A strong, dynamic midfielder who, like most Brazilians, gets forward but, unlike many Samba stars, is robust in the challenge.

Highly rated even before his Copa Libertadores success, Sandro - full name Sandro Ranieri Guimarães Cordeiro - is believed to have spurned Arsenal for Tottenham and will add quality to an already strong-looking midfield.

ℹ FACT FILE

BIRTH PLACE:	Riachinho, Brazil
BIRTH DATE:	March 15, 1989
POSITION:	Midfielder
HEIGHT:	1.87m (6ft 1in)
CLUBS:	Internacional, Tottenham

DID YOU KNOW?

As part of the deal to sign Sandro, Tottenham have also secured first option on all young players who emerge at Internacional, so expect plenty more young Brazilians arriving in North London in the future!

Laurent Koscielny

ℹ FACT FILE

BIRTH PLACE:	Tulle, France
BIRTH DATE:	September 10, 1985
POSITION:	Defender
HEIGHT:	1.86m (6ft 1in)
CLUBS:	Guingamp, Tours, Lorient, Arsenal

DID YOU KNOW?

Voted Ligue 2's most valuable player two seasons ago, Koscielny's rise has been rapid. In the space of four years he has gone from the French third division to Arenal's first-team squad!

Arsenal's attacking philosophy over recent years has often led to their backline feeling exposed and looking susceptible. Arsene Wenger has sought to address that - scrapping ageing stars Sol Campbell, William Gallas, Mikael Silvestre and unfancied Philippe Senderos.

Little-known prior to his arrival at the Emirates, Koscielny is the man charged with stepping into the breach.

A defender capable of roaming forward and comfortable on the ball, he will suit Arsenal's style of play. Despite being sent off on his Premier League debut against Liverpool, Koscielny is a talented defender.

If he can maintain that impression during the course of the season, he will make a mockery of those questioning his ability to make the 'big step up'.

CHAMPIONSHIP CAPTURES!

Big names head for second tier

Every summer there are a handful of Premier League players who drop down to the Championship.

Some have been frozen out at their club, like Coventry's Gary McSheffrey was at Birmingham; while others arrive on loan looking for first-team chances, as Tottenham's John Bostock has done with Hull City for season 2010-11.

Some move for the adventure, like Craig Bellamy's shock loan move to Cardiff City (read his profile on page 109 for more on that). Here are three more big name Championship signings...

David James

ℹ️ FACT FILE

BIRTH PLACE:	Welwyn Garden City, England
BIRTH DATE:	August 1, 1970
POSITION:	Holding midfielder
HEIGHT:	1.96m (6ft 5in)
CLUBS:	Watford, Liverpool, Aston Villa, West Ham, Man City, Portsmouth, Bristol City
INTERNATIONAL:	England

DID YOU KNOW?

James is the all-time Premier League appearance record holder, having made 573 top-flight appearances!

England's number one during the summer, City fans couldn't believe it when they heard that the giant stopper was heading to Ashton Gate.

Having been linked with Sunderland and Celtic, amongst others, James made the surprise decision to drop into the Championship to play for Bristol City - so he could be closer to his family in the South West.

Now 40, but still as physically fit as ever, James was one of the very few positives for Portsmouth fans in season 2009-10.

Having already seen Steve Coppell leave the club to be replaced by Keith Millen, the Robins can probably turn to James for advice on crisis management. Keen to lead the club to the Premier League, James will earn his new club points by himself.

Kris Boyd

ℹ️ FACT FILE

BIRTH PLACE:	Irvine, Scotland
BIRTH DATE:	August 18, 1983
POSITION:	Striker
HEIGHT:	1.83m (6ft 0in)
CLUBS:	Kilmarnock, Rangers, Middlesbrough
INTERNATIONAL:	Scotland

DID YOU KNOW?

Another record holder, Boyd is the SPL's all-time record goalscorer, usurping Celtic legend Henrik Larsson.

As prolific as they come, Boyd drew admiring glances from many clubs during the summer, not least because he was available on a free transfer.

Many had expected him to link up with former boss Alex McLeish at Birmingham City, but instead he opted for the Scottish revolution at Middlesbrough.

He will look to transfer his goal-scoring prowess to south of the border, in a Boro side heavily fancied for promotion, despite a slow start to the season.

Jason Koumas

ℹ️ FACT FILE

BIRTH PLACE:	Wrexham, Wales
BIRTH DATE:	September 25, 1979
POSITION:	Holding midfielder
HEIGHT:	1.78m (5ft 10in)
CLUBS:	Tranmere, West Brom, Cardiff, Wigan, Crdiff
INTERNATIONAL:	Wales

DID YOU KNOW?

Koumas' father is a Greek Cypriot chip shop owner and could've represented either Cyprus or Wales, internationally. Having grown up in Wales he opted to play for the Dragons.

A precocious talent as a youth at Tranmere Rovers, the classy attacking midfielder has been popular with fans at every club he has played for.

His £5m switch to Wigan wasn't been as effective as he'd have liked, disrupted by injury and a lack of first team chances. A loan switch to Cardiff appeared to be the perfect remedy.

It's the second time Koumas has been loaned to the Bluebirds, establishing himself as a cult hero during his first spell in 2006.

West Brom denied Koumas a permanent deal that summer, after the wizard was named in the Championship Team of the Year for the second time in his career.

After remaining with the Baggies he won that title again the following season, where he was also named Player of the Year, before moving on to Wigan.

With the arrival of fellow loanee Craig Bellamy, Cardiff established a core of star local players in their bid to be the first Welsh club to reach the Premier League.

LEAGUES ONE AND TWO ROUND-UP

The best transfer action from the lower leagues

League One

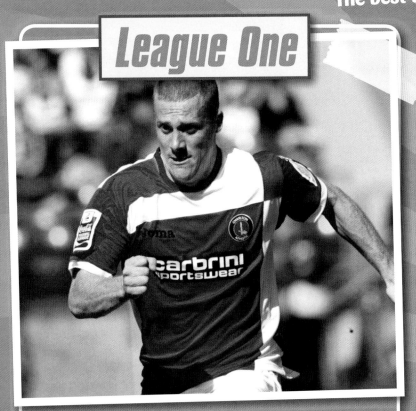

Much of summer 2010's focus on League One centred on the reshuffling taking place at Charlton Athletic.

Having lost captain Nicky Bailey to Middlesbrough for £1.4m and starlet Jonjo Shelvey to Liverpool for £1.7m, boss Phil Parkinson had a rebuilding job to undertake.

To cut costs he had to release 14 players, while sanctioning the £450,000 sale of Frazer Richardson to rivals Southampton.

In came Kyel Reid, Johnnie Jackson and Gary Doherty on free transfers. Strikers Pawel Abbott and Akpo Sodje arrived for nominal fees, while Parkinson dipped into the loan market - former Manchester United youth Lee Martin joining from Ipswich Town.

Elsewhere, there were some big name arrivals to the division. MK Dons' new manager Karl Robinson may only be 30, the youngest boss in the Football League, but he made an impact with the capture of Liverpool and Germany legend Dietmar Hamann.

The 36-year-old player-coach may be past his prime, but should still be able to have an impact at this level.

Relegated Sheffield Wednesday looked to bolster their chances of bouncing back to the Championship by landing Coventry City forward Clinton Morrison.

A goalscorer everywhere he has played, Republic of Ireland striker Morrison notched on his Owls debut.

Other notable arrivals to this division were former top-flight duo Jon Harley and Joey Gudjonsson.

Former Chelsea and Fulham defender Harley arrived at Notts County on a free transfer from Watford, while ex-Aston Villa midfielder Gudjonsson swapped Burnley for ambitious Huddersfield Town.

League Two

There were some prominent summer 2010 captures in the bottom tier of League football.

Promoted outfit Oxford United snared the surprise signing of the summer by landing former Chelsea defender Harry Worley from Leicester City.

Worley, still in his early 20s, has had a succession of loan spells in his career, including a season-long switch to Crewe in 2009-10.

Having failed to establish himself with Leicester, Worley convinced the club to tear up his contract so he could go in search of first-team football. He will be key to the Yellows in their bid to retain League status.

Relegated Gillingham were dealt a blow when they lost leading scorer Simeon Jackson to Championship side Norwich City, but reacted quickly to replace their talisman.

Their replacement was Northampton's Adebayo Akinfenwa, a hero at the Sixfields, who offers a physical force and goal-threat to lead the line.

He demonstrated this on his debut, heading home powerfully against Cheltenham. The onus will be on the big forward to replace Jackson's goals.

Other players arriving from higher divisions included Glen Little and Darren Moore.

Experienced winger Little has played in the Premier League with Bolton, Reading and Portsmouth, but was only a bit-part player for Sheffield United in the Championship last season. He arrived at Aldershot Town on a one-year deal.

Moore also has top tier experience in abundance, most memorably with West Brom, though he has been part of four sides that have won promotion to the Premier League.

The centre back arrived at Burton Albion from Barnsley, to be reunited with former Derby team-mate Paul Peschisolido.

SCOTTISH PREMIER SWITCHES

Transfer round-up from north of the border

Celtic

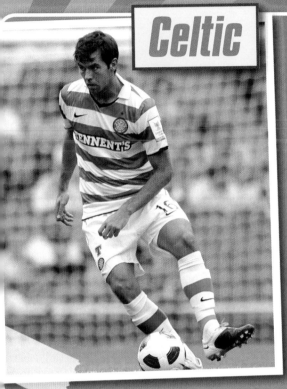

Manager Neil Lennon wasted no time in ripping up the squad he inherited from Tony Mowbray.

The Hoops lost seven times last season in a severely under-par campaign. Though they were knocked out of Champions League qualifying, things still look brighter at Parkhead following a reshuffle.

Star man Aiden McGeady completed a £9.5m move to Spartak Moscow, keeper Artur Boruc was off-loaded to Fiorentina for £1.5m, the same price captain Stephen McManus was allowed to join Middlesbrough for.

Various other bit-part players have also been moved on, making room for Lennon's influx of new talent.

The Bosman signing of Joe Ledley, one of Cardiff City's star performers last season, was shrewd, while Scunthorpe's aptly named Gary Hooper should ensure goals after a £2.4m switch.

Daryl Murphy, Charlie Mulgrew and Cha Du Ri all arrived on free transfers amongst a host of signings.

Rangers

Rangers had a difficult summer in 2010.

Stricken by their financial perils, Gers had to say goodbye to bright prospect Danny Wilson, the SPL's record goalscorer Kris Boyd and captain Kevin Thomson.

The club couldn't afford to keep on high earners such as DaMarcus Beasley and Nacho Novo, but were able to swoop for £4m striker Nikica Jelavic - their most expensive signing for eight seasons.

They also added out-of-favour Stoke City forward James Beattie (above) to bolster their attacking options.

Manager Walter Smith had to scour the market for loan signings and, if he can recruit more like Man City winger Vladimir Weiss, he will be hopeful of putting together a side capable of retaining their Scottish Premier League title.

With the experienced manager set to hand over the reins to assistant Ally McCoist at the end of the season, he'd love to sign off in style.

SHOOT LEGEND

FACT FILE

GARY WINSTON LINEKER

BIRTH DATE: November 30, 1960

BIRTH PLACE: Leicester, England

POSITION: Striker

HEIGHT: 1.80m (5ft 11in)

CLUBS:
Leicester City, Everton, Barcelona, Tottenham, Nagoya Grampus Eight

INTERNATIONAL:
England (80 caps, 48 goals)

Jimmy Greaves, Kevin Keegan, Alan Shearer, Michael Owen. England has produced some fine attackers, but few - not even the illustrious quartet above - can compare to Gary Lineker.

Now BBC TV's face of football coverage, he was once the face of English football full stop.

In an England shirt, only Sir Bobby Charlton out-scored him - by a solitary strike, over an extra 26 caps. Truly, Linker is one of the greatest goalscorers we've ever seen.

That is reflected at club level, where he is the only player to have won the English Golden Boot with three different clubs.

He also remains the only Englishman to have won the

Golden Boot in a World Cup finals, achieving the honour as he fired England to the 1986 quarter finals in Mexico; before Diego Maradona's 'Hand of God' intervened.

Those performances led to a £2.2m switch to Spanish giants Barcelona, where Lineker made an instant impact - bagging a hat-trick against arch-rivals Real Madrid to endear himself to the fans, en route to 21 goals in his debut season.

74

Despite being a popular figure at the Nou Camp, Lineker fell out of favour when Terry Venables was replaced by Johan Cruyff as coach.

The Dutch manager preferred to play Lineker in midfield, where he was less effective, and a return to England with Tottenham was inevitable – where he continued to score, leading Spurs to the 1991 FA Cup.

Though he had a successful club career, it was in the international arena that Lineker really established himself – part of the England side that came so tragically close to the 1990 World Cup Final.

Since that semi-final penalty defeat to West Germany in 1990, the Three Lions have never looked like delivering the success the whole country craves, nor a goalscorer in the ilk of Lineker.

➡ ENGLAND HIGHS AND LOWS
Lineker's career with the national team

➡ 1986 WORLD CUP
England v Poland

The goal that Lineker describes as changing his whole career. The then-Everton frontman put England ahead against Poland to end a personal goal-drought and to give his international side a chance of progression – having lost and drawn their first two group games.

He went on to bag the second quickest World Cup hat-trick of all time and take the tournament's Golden Boot, earning him a move to Barcelona.

➡ 1990 WORLD CUP
England v West Germany

Having equalised to take the game into extra time, and subsequently penalties, Lineker converted England's first effort of the semi-final shoot-out. Infamous misses from Stuart Pearce and Chris Waddle knocked England out of the tournament in heartbreaking fashion. Germany went on to lift the trophy. It should have been England. Instead, Bobby Robson's men got the Fair Play trophy!

➡ 1992 FRIENDLY
England v Brazil

The one moment that could've changed history. Gary Lineker stepped up to take a penalty, knowing that scoring it would put him level with Sir Bobby Charlton at the top of England's scoring charts.

That he missed is a travesty, and remains the only blight on his career – where he famously never got booked or sent off!

THE FUTURE OF ENGLAND

Theo Walcott

ⓘ KEY STATS

POSITION: Striker
BIRTH DATE: March 16, 1989
BIRTH PLACE: Stanmore, Middlesex
HEIGHT: 1.75m (5ft 9in)
CURRENT CLUB: Arsenal

Walcott is the speed king. Once he is up and running there are very few players who can catch him. They may even have to foul him and give away a free-kick or penalty to stop him. Can play wide or as a striker.

For many players in the England squad, the World Cup finals of 2010 was their last chance to shine at the biggest football competition on the planet.

But there were few bright spots, few highlights and no praise for the players who pulled on the Three Lions' shirts.

Four games, one unconvincing win, two draws and a 4-1 thrashing at the hands of Germany in the Round of 16 saw Fabio Capello's side head home to a barrage of criticism.

The side had breezed through qualification and the whole of England expected great things at South Africa

2010. It wasn't even whispered quietly: the hope was that England might just be able to get their hands on that famous trophy for a second time, and the first in 44 years.

They didn't and now it's time to look to the future: to the players who might just offer England some hope…

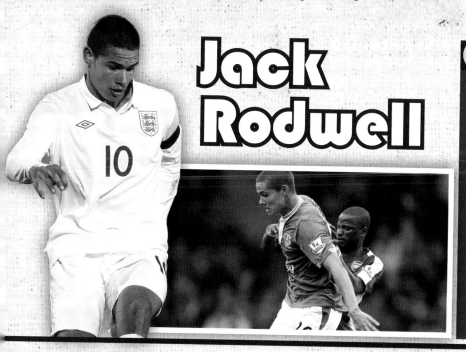

Jack Rodwell

ⓘ KEY STATS

POSITION: Midfielder
BIRTH DATE: March 11, 1991
BIRTH PLACE: Southport, Merseyside
HEIGHT: 1.88m (6ft 2in)
CURRENT CLUB: Everton

Fergie fancied taking him to Manchester United but Everton were quick to add five years to his contract. A defensive midfielder who has been touted as a possible centre-half, he's also shown that he is just as capable in an attacking role.

ⓘ KEY STATS

POSITION: Defender
BIRTH DATE: November 22, 1989
BIRTH PLACE: Greenwich, London
HEIGHT: 1.93m (6ft 4in)
CURRENT CLUB: Manchester United

A fairytale rise from non-League football to Premier League reserves for Fulham, a handful of first-team appearances, praise and a move to Manchester United, all in under two years! Now the central defender - whose transfer could cost as much as £14m - is set to be groomed by the best boss around. The future looks good.

Chris Smalling

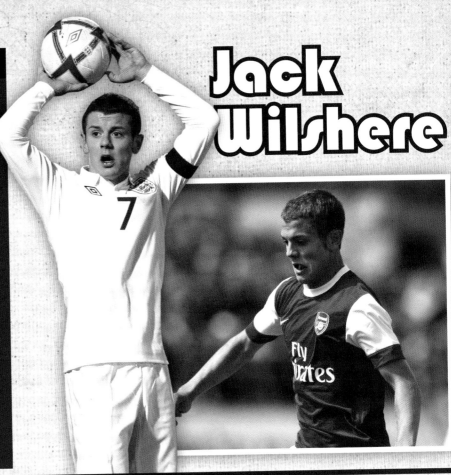

Jack Wilshere

KEY STATS

POSITION: Midfielder
BIRTH DATE: January 1, 1992
BIRTH PLACE: Stevenage, Hertfordshire
HEIGHT: 1.7m (5ft 7in)
CURRENT CLUB: Arsenal

One Englishman that Arsene Wenger is highly unlikely to allow to leave Arsenal. His loan at Bolton for the second-half of 2009-10 confirmed the attacking midfielder's confidence and ability. Had been touted as a surprise call-up for South Africa 2010, but that was never really going to happen. Still only a teenager, Wilshere fits perfectly into Arsenal's style of play, though it may be another season or two before he establishes himself in the first-team.

Joe Hart

KEY STATS

POSITION: Goalkeeper
BIRTH DATE: April 19, 1987
BIRTH PLACE: Shrewsbury, Shropshire
HEIGHT: 1.91m (6ft 3in)
CURRENT CLUB: Manchester City

We know - keepers are better as they get older. Forget about that in the case of Hart. He's good now! He more than proved his abilities at Birmingham during season 2009-10 and it's now time to install him in the international set-up. Cool, composed and confident between the posts, the stopper has an aura around him that belies his age. Surely England's long term number one.

Gabriel Agbonlahor

Like Walcott, the Aston Villa man has speed. But he also has that swagger about him that most good strikers need – and he also has the power to push off strong challenges from defenders. Established as first-choice at Villa, 'Gabby' offers an excellent all-round threat.

...and one player who went to South Africa 2010 and proved himself

James Milner

A star at Under-21 level, Milner has now proved himself ready for the seniors. A livewire performer who just never stops contributing to a game. Has played at full-back, wide left and right, striker and central midfield. And he's done well in all roles. But it's in the centre where he influences play or wide right where he can zoom past defenders and deliver amazing passes into the box.

CLASSIC IMAGE

GERMANY 1 ENGLAND 5 SEPTEMBER 2001

One goal down in Munich in a World Cup 2002 qualifier, things did not look good for England. But Michael Owen equalised and just before half-time Steven Gerrard scored his first senior goal for his country. Owen went on to notch a hat-trick – and even Emile Heskey got in on the scoring act! It was only the second time ever that Germany had lost a World Cup qualifier on home soil and only the second time they had been beaten by England since the 1966 World Cup Final.

Deutschland
England
1 : 5

Olympiastadion München
01 SEP. 2001

TOP TRIVIA

LAUGH, CRY OR JUST BE AMAZED AT THE WORLD OF FOOTBALL

MESSI'S RUBBISH

Lionel Messi reckons he lives up to his name. The Argentina ace admits that his club car is full of rubbish! And don't expect to have a feast if you are invited round to his pad for a meal – he sends out for a takeaway!

EAR OF GOD?

An earring belonging to legendary Argentina star Maradona was bought for £20,000.

Police in Italy seized the item of jewellery because the former midfielder owed their taxman a load of cash.

It was bought by Palermo striker Fabrizio Miccoli who said he hoped to give the earring back to Maradona, a player he idolizes.

TAKING THE BISCUIT

Blackpool arrived in the Premier League with the smallest ground and one of the smallest budgets.

So it will come as no surprise to learn that their worst trainer every week also has to suffer one of the smaller forfeits.

Their poorest performer on the training ground every week has to fork out a fiver to buy his team- mates biscuits!

TATT'S NO GOOD!

Spare a thought for super fan Kirk Bradley. The Man City nut decided his favourite Man City side was doing so well he would have a special Champions League tattoo on his arm. The only problem is... the side failed to even qualify for Europe's biggest club tournament and he had to decide to change it from "winners 2011" to the year they do lift the trophy...if they do!

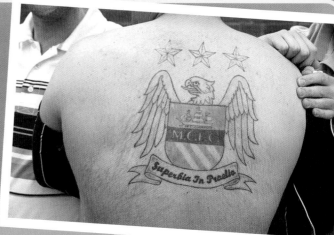

DRIVING FORCE

A football club that ran out of cash paid its players in cars. Nistru Otaci in Moldova gave eight of their stars VWs and then ordered more for other players.

FRENCH KICK

A football fan's chances of winning £1.65m went out of the window when France exited the World Cup.

The Englishman had bet £110,000 on them winning South Africa 2010 and was stunned when Thierry Henry's side exited at the group stage.

NANI THE HANDYMAN

Need a bit if DIY doing around the house? Well drop a line to Man United midfielder Nani!

Most Old Trafford stars just call on the club's in-house team of Mr Fixits if they need something doing.

But not Nani. You are more likely to spot him in Wickes or Homebase buying a few tools and accessories to sort out his own flash home just down the road from boss Sir Alex Ferguson.

In fact his team-mates are so impressed with the Portugal star that they nicknamed him Bob the Builder!

WHAT A SURPRISE... NOT... WELL MAYBE NOT!

A survey has shown that less than half of Manchester United's fans live within ten miles of their stadium.

The majority of Stoke City supporters - 82 per cent - live near the Potters' ground.

Meanwhile, Old Trafford has been voted the friendliest football stadium in the country - with Millwall's New Den the unfriendliest.

Next on the friendly fans list were Arsenal's Emirates Stadium, Liverpool's Anfield, Chelsea's Stamford Bridge and St. James' Park, Newcastle.

Arsenal

ⓘ **FACT FILE**

THEO WALCOTT

BIRTH DATE: March 16, 1989

BIRTH PLACE: Stanmore, West London

POSITION: Striker

HEIGHT: 1.75m (5ft 9in)

CLUBS: Southampton, Arsenal

INTERNATIONAL: England

The country was stunned when Theo Walcott was named in England's squad for the 2006 World Cup finals never having played a Premier League game.

By the time the squad for the 2010 finals in South Africa was announced the forward had clocked up more than 80 Premier League appearances for Arsenal... and a number of fans were just as surprised when he was omitted from Fabio Capello's final 23.

Theo was just 17-years-old when he was named for Germany 2006 following his £12m move from Southampton to the Gunners. Walcott never got his backside off the subs bench during that tournament.

Injury did restrict him during season 2009-10 but his lightning pace and his ability to shoot past defenders appeared to make him a favourite for South Africa.

If nothing else, he could offer a high impact sub with the ability to change a game. And how they needed that during the finals!

But Capello allowed Walcott to disappear on his holidays and there were reports the Italian wasn't happy that the player stuck to the position he was told to play.

➲ WHAT HIS CLUB BOSS SAYS

Arsene Wenger
Arsenal Manager

"If you have to look for a weakness in [Lionel] Messi you would say it is his ability to run without the ball, behind the defender. When he takes the ball to his feet he's like a Ferrari. But Theo is more a guy who has the timing to run off the ball and that is something that is difficult to find."

TAKE YOUR PICK...

Theo Walcott's world of confusion

⮕ THEO WALCOTT ON...

World Cup 2006
"Looking back, 2006 did come too quickly for me. It did create pressure and it was surreal being there at the World Cup with some great players who had been playing for years in the Premier League and I hadn't played one game in the division."

World Cup 2010
"I was very disappointed not to be included in the squad going out to South Africa, but I completely respected Mr Capello's decision."

Handling early success
"I have had to cope with a lot of attention and a lot of pressure from a very young age and people haven't always made allowances for my inexperience. But I have learnt to deal with it."

the good bits
"One of the highlights of my career so far was to become the youngest player to have scored a hat-trick for England, against Croatia. But I don't want to be remembered always for that."

High speed
"I had two tests between five and 15 metres and five and 40 metres and broke Thierry Henry's two records. I am quicker!"

His club boss Arsene Wenger
"He loves his job and shows passion for the game. He shows tremendous respect for the players and has brought us some brilliant players over the years."

Winning with Arsenal
"I think we need to do the dirty things right. Sometimes it's not just about pretty football. We need to grind out results sometimes and get points. Manchester United and Chelsea do the dirty work and take their chances as well. We need to be more cutting in the last third."

His playing position
"The boss said he will start me up front now and then. That's my natural position but I'd play anywhere for the team. He believes in me but I have still got a lot to do. The experience I have had in the last few years will definitely help.

His Arsenal hopes
"Instead of finishing fourth we want to be challenging for titles. The Champions League is one of the best tournaments around. Every team is difficult, every team needs to be feared and should be given respect."

⮕ WHY DIDN'T HE GO IN 2010?

Fabio Capello
The England boss who overlooked Walcott

"I know that Theo Walcott was really important in the qualification games for the World Cup. But after the operation on the shoulder, he did not play in a lot of games. He's not the same player that we knew before this injury. I was really upset for him but we had to choose the best players at the best moment."

SHOOT
The voice of football

THE BOSS

WENG
WOB
WHEN ARSENE G

FACT FILE

Arsène Wenger

Birth date: October 22, 1949

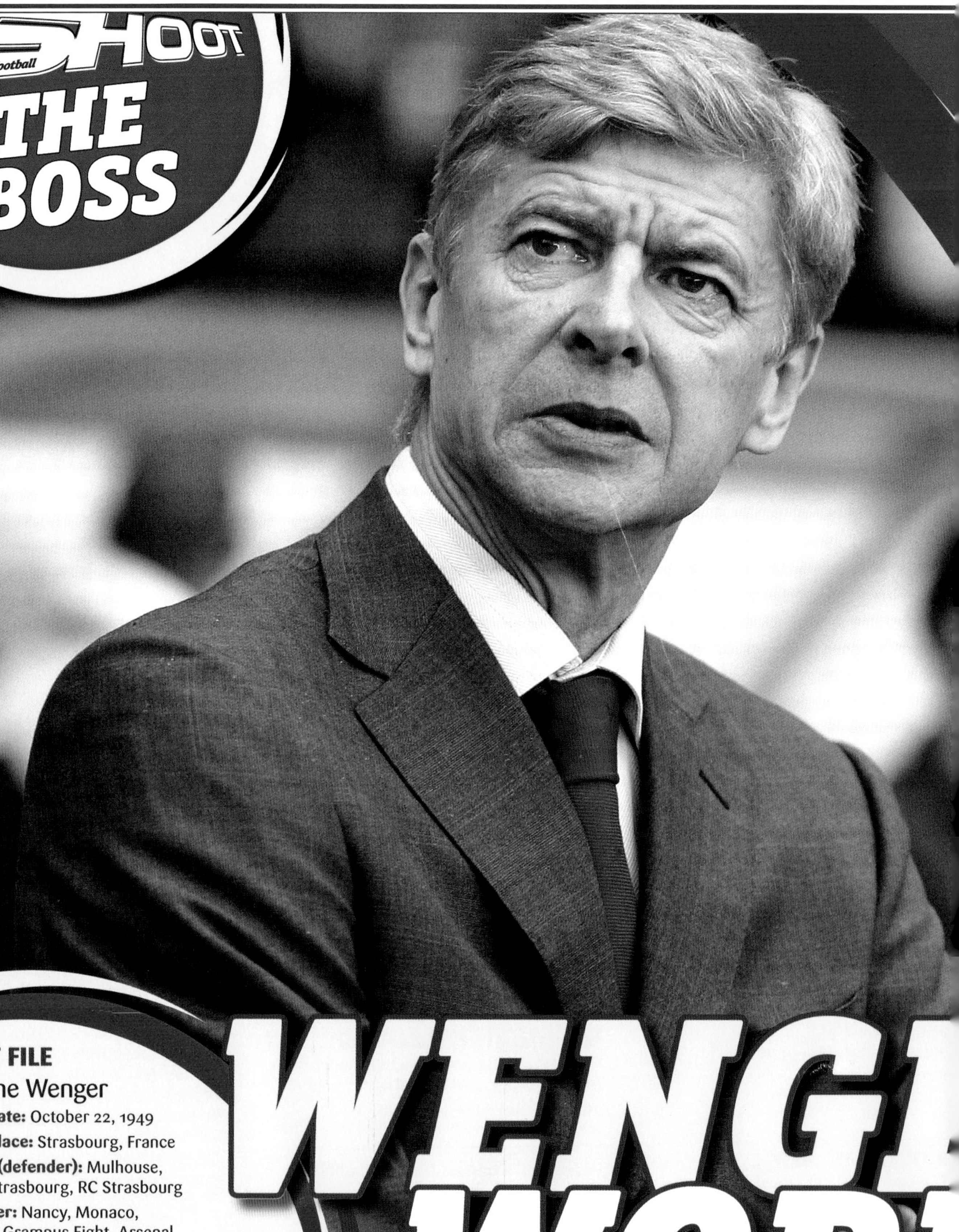

Birth place: Strasbourg, France

Player (defender): Mulhouse, ASPV Strasbourg, RC Strasbourg

Manager: Nancy, Monaco, Nagoya Grampus Eight, Arsenal

What he's won:
Player: Ligue One (Strasbourg)
Manager: French Cup, Ligue One (Monaco); Emperor's Cup, J-League Super Cup (Grampus); Premier League 1998, 2002, 2004, FA Cup 1998, 2002, 2003, 2005, Community Shield, 1998, 1999, 2002, 2004 (Arsenal).

Did you know?
Match of the Day presenter and former England striker Gary Lineker played under Wenger during his time at Grampus in Japan.

He's been dubbed The Professor but when Arsene Wenger gets wound up about something he's more like the Mad Scientist!

We always thought the Arsenal boss was the quiet, studious type, the big thinker of English football.

Although just recently he's started to become very animated when things don't go his way – and we love it, just love it, when he proves he can get as wild as the rest of us about football!

But Arsene does have quite a lot of previous form for throwing his toys out of the pram...

December 2005
One of the first guys he refused to shake hands with was Jose Mourinho. Their simmering relationship wasn't helped by the Special One accusing Wenger of being a "voyeur" who liked to watch people!
Wobble rating: 5

April 2006
Stewards had to separate the Arsenal boss and then Spurs manager Martin Jol when they came face to face on the touchline. Jol was urging his players to attack when two Gunners were on the floor injured.
Wobble rating: 8

November 2006
He wasn't happy when West Ham scored a late winner and pushed Hammers boss Alan Pardew. Then he refused to shake hands. He was landed with a £10,000 FA fine.
Wobble rating: 6

August 2009
Wenger went a bit wobbly during the game at Old Trafford which Arsenal lost 2-1. Just 30 seconds from the final whistle he lost the plot at an offside decision and ref Mike Dean ordered him into the stand. Top man even stood among the United fans!
Wobble rating: 8

October 2009
If he couldn't get excited at the 3-0 home win over Spurs he might as well pack in! This was top drawer though – an attempt at doing the Crouch Robot dance on the touchline at the final whistle, and earlier a jacket throwing incident when he couldn't get messages through to his team.
Wobble rating: 9.5

➔ Professor **Arsene Wenger** on his first day at Highbury on September 26, 1996

December 2009
Arsene got a bit... well you know the word, when his side were thrashed 3-0 at Man City in the League Cup and refused to shake the hand of Eastlands boss Mark Hughes. The head Gunner said it was nothing to do with the defeat but Hughes' improper behaviour.
Wobble rating: 7

Best of all...
Is the war of words and often hilarious incidents involving Man United chief Sir Alex Ferguson and Wenger.

There was, of course, the infamous pizza flinging incident of 2004 in which Fergie was hit by a flying slice. Wenger was not to blame!

Here are two of their best quotes...

Fergie on Wenger:
"They say he's an intelligent man, right? Speaks five languages! I have a 15-year-old boy from the Ivory Coast who speaks five languages,"

Wenger on Fergie:
"I will never answer any question any more about this man. He doesn't interest me and doesn't matter to me at all. I will never answer to any provocation from him any more."

Since Sir Alex passed the age of 68 and Wenger has now reached 60, they appear to have mellowed towards each other though and are more likely to get involved in a heated discussion about red wine.

R'S
LERS
A BIT CRAZY...

Arsenal

YOUNG GUNNERS

Wenger's budding stars hoping to breakthrough

Having agreed a three-year extension to his contract, which would take his stay at the North London club to 17 years, Arsene Wenger is hoping for a bright future at Arsenal.

Renowned across the world as a coach who likes to build young, talented sides that play attractive football, Wenger is ushering through another generation of exciting youths.

Having been responsible for the emergence of world-class players such as Marc Overmars, Thierry Henry and Cesc Fabregas, Wenger's pedigree is undoubted.

For season 2010-11 he has looked to promote one of the Arsenal Academy's most exciting prospects, Jack Wilshere, to the Gunners' first-team.

Alongside fellow England youngsters Theo Walcott and Kieran Gibbs, Wilshere is spearheading something of a refreshingly English revolution in North London.

With captain Fabregas seemingly destined for a return to boyhood club Barcelona at some point in the not-so-distant future, much is expected of Wilshere – with many supporters hoping to see him prove his worth as Fabregas's long-term successor.

⊃ THOMAS CRUISE

The defender with a celebrity name, there are high hopes surrounding the future of Cruise. Having achieved success at an international level with the Under-17s and Under-19s, as well as the Arsenal Academy, first-team appearances for the Gunners will be next on the agenda.

⊃ CARLOS VELA

An incredibly skilful forward, 21-year-old Vela is already a dynamic option from the bench. Despite it being early days in his Arsenal career, Vela has already notched the goal that was voted as the second greatest goal ever scored by the Gunners! That memorable lob against Sheffield United in the League Cup sums up the Mexico forward's style of play perfectly.

⊃ JACK WILSHERE

Still only 18, Wilshere has been touted as a bright talent for some time now.

Season 2009-10's five month loan at Bolton offered the youngster a stage on which to substantiate the hype, and he didn't disappoint.

Making 14 Premier League appearances with the Trotters, Wilshere was rewarded with an England call-up in August 2010, coming on as a substitute to make his national team debut.

And Fabio Capello hasn't been the only manager to sit up and take note of the prodigal talent; with Arsene Wenger fast-tracking the midfielder into Arsenal's first-team.

Wilshere looks ready to cement himself as part of the Gunners' squad, a player with the world at his feet.

NAME: Jack Andrew Wilshere
BIRTH DATE: January 1, 1992
BIRTH PLACE: Stevenage
POSITION: Attacking midfielder
HEIGHT: 1.78m (5ft 10in)
CLUBS: Arsenal, Bolton (loan)
INTERNATIONAL: England

DID YOU KNOW?
Despite playing for Arsenal, Wilshere is passionate about another team in London – West Ham!

➲ KIERAN GIBBS

Anyone trying to oust Gael Clichy from a starting line-up would have to be immensely talented to stand a chance.

That the France full back has such an able deputy in Gibbs is often credited as the main reason behind his excellent displays of recent seasons.

Having a talent like Gibbs waiting in the wings is certainly keeping Clichy on his toes.

When Clichy has been injured, and Gibbs has been given an extended first-team run, we've seen that Arsenal could have England's next great left back on their books – following current incumbent Ashley Cole at Arsenal.

A part of the England Under-21 side that reached the 2009 European Championships Final, it won't be long before Gibbs is pushing former team-mate Cole for his international berth.

NAME: Kieran James Ricardo Gibbs
BIRTH DATE: September 26, 1989
BIRTH PLACE: Lambeth, London
POSITION: Left back
HEIGHT: 1.80m (5ft 11in)
CLUBS: Arsenal, Norwich (loan)
INTERNATIONAL: England

DID YOU KNOW?
Gibbs started his career as part of the Wimbledon Youth Academy but, when the club disbanded and was reformed as the MK Dons, Gibbs opted for Arsenal.

➲ THEO WALCOTT

Signed for an initial £9m as a 16-year-old, earning an England call-up prior to his Arsenal debut, it seems like Walcott has been around forever.

At 21, the speedy winger still has plenty of time to improve, and his shock exclusion from England's 2010 World Cup squad will provide him with the incentive to do so.

The youngest-ever hat-trick scorer for England, after THAT performance against Croatia in 2008, some had criticised Walcott for a lack of improvement.

His three-goal haul against Blackpool at the start of season 20010-11 disproved critics who labelled his star turn as a one-off.

He appears to have taken all criticism in his stride and has returned for the campaign looking sharper and fresher than ever before.

NAME: Theo James Walcott
BIRTH DATE: March 16, 1989
BIRTH PLACE: Stanmore, Harrow
POSITION: Striker, winger
HEIGHT: 1.75m (5ft 9in)
CLUBS: Southampton, Arsenal
INTERNATIONAL: England

DID YOU KNOW?
Walcott could've been wearing blue for season 20010-11! Theo left the Swindon Town Youth Academy after only six months, rejecting an offer from Chelsea and instead joining Southampton. Saints have now earned £12m from his transfer.

➲ JAY EMMANUEL-THOMAS

Shone during loan spells with Blackpool and Doncaster in the Championship last season.

The powerful player, who can be deployed in either midfield or attack, was captain of Arsenal's double-winning youth side in 2009.

➲ AARON RAMSEY

Wowed the Premier League with his performances prior to a broken leg in February 2010, and much is expected of the Wales midfielder upon his return.

Described by Wenger as "an offence-minded Roy Keane", Ramsey has the ability to go to the very top.

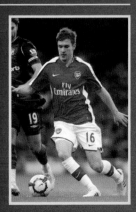

IN THE RED
ARSENAL'S NEW BOYS

➲ SEBASTIEN SQUILLACI

Arsenal's downfall in 2009-10 was their defence. They conceded more goals than not only top two Chelsea and Manchester United, but also Aston Villa and Liverpool.

In the top eight, only Tottenham and Liverpool lost more games – Arsenal's defensive problems needed to be addressed during the summer.

Alongside emerging talent Laurent Koscielny, Wenger brought in compatriot Squillaci to steady the ship.

The 30-year-old has title-winning experience from his time with Lyon and helped Sevilla to Copa del Rey success last season.

The £6.5m signing meant that Wenger could now field an all French speaking backline. Bacary Sagna, Koscielny and Gael Clichy are all French, while Johan Djourou, Emmanuel Eboue, Alex Song and Thomas Vermaelen all have French as their first language.

England youngster Kieran Gibbs is the only exception!

Squillaci had an injury hit campaign in Seville, but was expected to be relied upon to bring experience to the new-look defensive line-up; replacing the departing elder statesmen, Campbell and Gallas.

BIRTH DATE: August 11, 1980

BIRTH PLACE: Toulon, France

POSITION: Centre back

HEIGHT: 1.85m (6ft 1in)

CLUBS: Toulon, Monaco, Ajaccio (loan), Lyon, Sevilla, Arsenal

INTERNATIONAL: France

DID YOU KNOW?
Squillaci was a significant part of the Monaco side that reached the 2004 Champions League Final; scoring an all-important away goal against Real Madrid in the quarter-finals.

Renowned for his low-key transfer activity, Arsene Wenger had an unusually busy summer in 2010.

Keen to bolster the side that, although it finished third, was well adrift of the top two, Wenger has reshuffled his pack somewhat.

Defence was his priority, where the likes of Philippe Senderos, William Gallas, Sol Campbell and Mikael Silvestre all headed for pastures new.

Croatia forward Eduardo was off-loaded to Shakhtar Donetsk and midfield talent Fran Merida opted for a Spanish return with Atletico Madrid

With space freed up both in his squad and on his wage bill, Wenger moved to strengthen his squad.

Alongside Laurent Koscielny (profile page 70), here are some of the players charged with transforming the Gunners into title contenders once again.

⊃ MAROUANE CHAMAKH

Chamakh's transfer to Arsenal was speculated about for over a year. Having had an offer of around £7m turned down in August 2009, Arsene Wenger declared any possible deal for the forward as 'dead'.

Less than four months later, Chamakh had signed a pre-contract agreement to join Arsenal on a Bosman free.

That signing may well turn out to be the deal of the season. A player that attracted an £18m offer from West Ham last summer, Chamakh fits into the Arsenal style of play perfectly.

An attacker that likes to drift wide and engage in the build up play, Chamakh is excellent technically and offers a rare aerial threat for the Gunners.

Not the most prolific striker, Chamakh will hope to up his goal ante at the Emirates. Having scored in just his second game for Arsenal, Wenger was hopeful that his main signing would maintain that form during his debut Premier League campaign.

BIRTH DATE: January 10, 1984
BIRTH PLACE: Tonneins, France
POSITION: Forward
HEIGHT: 1.88m (6ft 2in)
CLUBS: Bordeaux, Arsenal
INTERNATIONAL: Morocco

DID YOU KNOW?
Having joined Bordeaux's youth system while at high school, Chamakh still went on to achieve an accounting qualification alongside his footballing career.

91

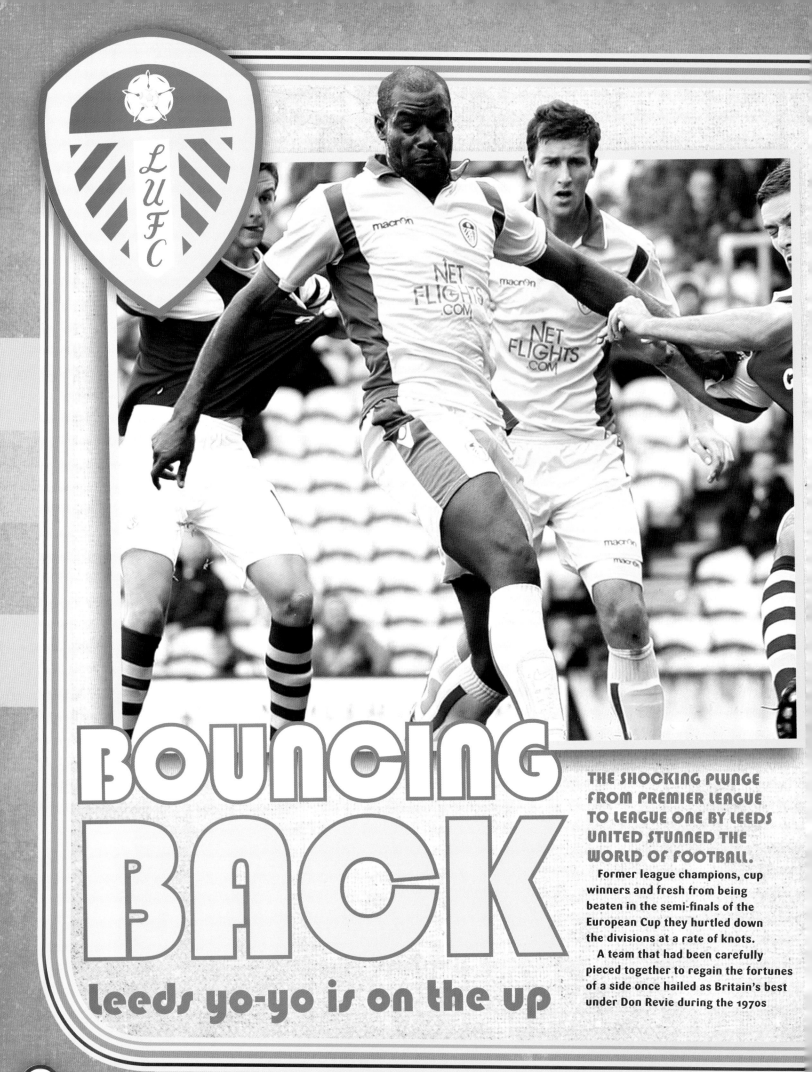

BOUNCING BACK

leeds yo-yo is on the up

THE SHOCKING PLUNGE FROM PREMIER LEAGUE TO LEAGUE ONE BY LEEDS UNITED STUNNED THE WORLD OF FOOTBALL.

Former league champions, cup winners and fresh from being beaten in the semi-finals of the European Cup they hurtled down the divisions at a rate of knots.

A team that had been carefully pieced together to regain the fortunes of a side once hailed as Britain's best under Don Revie during the 1970s had to be dismantled as crippling financial burdens hit home.

The last season of the old Division One, before the Premier League kicked off for 1992-93, saw Howard Wilkinson manage Leeds to the title with the likes of Gordon Strachan, Eric Cantona and David Batty in his side.

Things still looked good for a few years, especially when former Arsenal and Republic of Ireland midfield David O'Leary took control in 1998.

The lowest they finished in the league during his four years in charge was fifth and he got them to the semi-finals of the Champions League in 2001.

Failure to qualify for that competition in 2002 saw him get the boot and then the problems began...

Amidst stories that chairman Peter Ridsdale had ploughed a fortune into buying a fishtank for his boardroom, Leeds hit a financial crisis.

They had taken out loans against future TV deals and being in Europe. First to go was Rio Ferdinand to arch-rivals Man United for £30m.

It wasn't long afterwards that the likes of Jonathan Woodgate, Lee Bowyer, Nigel Martyn, Robbie Fowler, Robbie Keane and Harry Kewell were also on their bikes.

The crunch came at the end of season 2003-04 when Leeds were relegated whilst under the caretaker-manager charge of former Elland Road hero Eddie Gray.

Kevin Blackwell was brought in from Sheffield United but even more players left, including James Milner, Paul Robinson, Alan Smith and Mark Viduka. The club's ground and training ground were also sold off.

START OF THE RE-BIRTH

Kevin Blackwell kept the team mid-table during their first relegation year but they failed in the play-off final after their second season in the Championship.

Blackwell didn't last long into their third season in the lower tier, and former Newcastle coach John Carver couldn't turn the team around.

Chairman Ken Bates installed his ex-Stamford Bridge captain, Dennis Wise, as manager.

With a ten-point deduction for going into voluntary liquidation Wise had little chance of saving them from the drop into League One - the first time they had slumped to the third tier.

A further 15-points deduction and a slump in form saw Wise quit and his replacement, former player Gary McAllister, took Leeds to a play-off place. Again, they were beaten in the final, this time by Yorkshire neighbours Doncaster.

McAllister was sacked before Christmas the following season to be replaced by Yorkshire-born former Leeds player Simon Grayson, who had quit as manager of Blackpool.

Eight straight wins at the start of 2009-10 made Leeds favourites for promotion but after a shaky patch as the campaign neared an end their hopes of going up started to look unsure.

As it turned out, they needed to win on the last day of the season at home to Bristol Rovers. A goal down and a man sent-off before half-time things did not look good.

But then Jermaine Beckford, whose goals had shot them up the league earlier in the year, scored the second of the two goals to give them a 2-1 victory, take his tally to 31 for the season and guarantee their promotion.

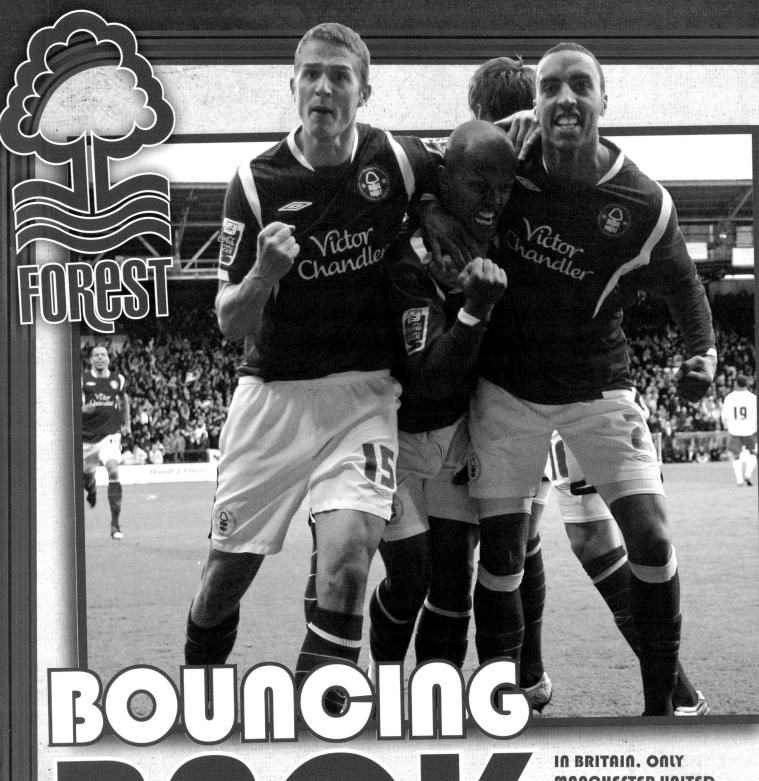

FOREST

BOUNCING BACK

from European Cup to League One (and back)

IN BRITAIN, ONLY MANCHESTER UNITED AND LIVERPOOL HAVE A BETTER RECORD THAN NOTTINGHAM FOREST IN THE EUROPEAN CUP.

The famous Forest side that won back-to-back European Cups was formed entirely of players from the United Kingdom and is one of only two teams - Porto being the other - to boast a 100% final success rate in Europe's premier competition.

So when, in 2005, Forest became the only former European Cup winners to be relegated to the third tier of their national league, it sent shockwaves around Europe.

Having lost their Premier League status in 1999, David Platt spent in excess of £12m trying to get the club to bounceback at the first time of asking. But when those expensive imports failed to deliver the goods, coupled with ITV Digital's collapse, Forest faced financial ruin.

That they staved off dropping down a tier until 2005 was some achievement, but it was a far cry from the halcyon days of the late 1970s.

THE GLORY DAYS

Forest had earned promotion to the top tier of English football in 1977 and followed that up with a surprise First Division title at the first time of asking. If that left fans of the Tricky Trees floating on air, then the next couple of seasons would have them mastering the art of flight!

They followed their surprise championship by winning the European Cup, just the third English side to do so, and then successfully defended it the following season, too!

Sandwiched between three Liverpool wins, it formed a miraculous stretch of five successive English champions of Europe - a feat only matched by Real Madrid's five straight wins in the 1960s.

That famous Forest side also won three League Cups, the European Super Cup, the Charity Shield and reached an FA Cup Final.

Under magic manager Brian Clough they enjoyed the best spell in their history. His 18-year reign came to an end, however, with disaster - the club suffering relegation from the newly formed Premier League in 1993.

After yo-yoing between the two divisions for some time, Forest found themselves in League One - the successes of yester-year distant.

THE RETURN JOURNEY

Colin Calderwood eventually led Forest back to the Championship, finishing as runners-up in the 2008 season. His side struggled to adapt after their promotion, though, and looked set for an instant return to League One.

With Calderwood relieved of his duties, Forest turned to wily Scot Billy Davies, who had taken rivals Derby to the Premier League two years previous.

After winning five of his first six games at the helm, the doom and gloom surrounding the City Ground lifted. From relegation certainties, Davies' side secured their survival with a game to spare.

Much like the Clough era, what was to come next was unexpected. Forest started the new campaign with a 20-match unbeaten run that ultimately propelled the side into promotion contenders.

An inexplicable loss of form towards the end of the campaign denied the team an automatic promotion berth, but did at least give them a play-off tie against unfancied surprise package Blackpool.

Ian Holloway's men shocked Forest and left them facing another year outside of the top-flight, stretching their absence to at least 12 seasons. Amongst the favourites for promotion in 2010-11, Forest's story is far from over...

CONTROVERSIAL. CHARISMATIC. CLOUGHY...

Rightly or wrongly most, if not all, of Forest's success is accredited to their now legendary manager, Brian Clough.

An incredible goalscorer during his playing days - notching 251 goals in just 274 games at club level - Clough seemed to possess a unique ability to provoke the best from his sides.

He took Derby County from the doldrums of Division Two to league champions and the European Cup semi-finals, where only a controversial defeat to Juventus denied the Rams progression to the final.

A man true to his principles, Clough walked away from the club after a lack of board backing.

He was famous for his outspoken comments, his single-minded nature and for being hard but fair.

When he arrived at Nottingham Forest, after brief, unsuccessful stints with Brighton and Leeds, Clough again found himself with a side struggling in Division Two.

In just his second full season at the helm, he earned Forest promotion back to the top-flight. What followed is now the stuff of legend - something Clough, the first inductee to the English Hall of Fame, certainly is.

PSYCHO POWER!

THERE WAS NOTHING FLASH ABOUT STUART PEARCE AS A PLAYER – JUST GOOD SOLID, RELIABLE, DEPENDABLE AND COMMITTED DEFENDING.

He was the type of guy you would want in your side. When he was missing for England or any of his club sides the teams were definitely weaker.

Pearce wasn't dubbed Psycho for nothing! He was one of those players who you could expect to lay his life on the line for the cause, go into tackles as if his life depended on it and defend like there was no tomorrow.

After leaving Newcastle where boss Ruud Gullit regularly and surprisingly overlooked him, Pearce played on at West Ham and then Manchester City until 2002.

When he hung up his boots he became a coach at City under Kevin Keegan – who had used him as an England player for a Euro 2000 qualifier. Pearce's last England appearance was in 1999.

When Keegan departed as City manager in 2005 Pearce took over. Just over two years later was sacked after the side had flirted with relegation.

He was already in charge of England Under-21s, a job he had done part-time whilst holding down his club position. He became full-time shortly after his sacking at City.

Incoming England boss Fabio Capello not only retained his Under-21 coach but also pulled Pearce into the senior coaching set-up, appointing him as one of his close backroom team.

Capello insisted that the FA extend Pearce's Under-21 contract – which they did – and there have even been suggestions that the Italian hopes to have groomed the former left-back as his successor ready for when he does leave the senior Three Lions post.

"I think it is really important that [goalkeeping coach] Ray Clemence and Stuart Pearce work with me because they are English," said Capello. "For me it is really important that some of my staff are English coaches."

CLASSIC IMAGE

GOING PSYCHO 1996

The clenched fists, the open mouth, the roar – Stuart Pearce celebrates his penalty shoot-out winner for England against Spain at Euro 96. Pearce had missed a spot-kick during the 1990 World Cup semi-final shoot-out with Germany. To walk up to the spot again in the Euro quarter-finals took real bottle! This time Pearce smashed the ball with venom past the Spain keeper. "All I was thinking when I took the penalty was to hit the ball cleanly and where I wanted it to go," he said afterwards.

CLASSIC IMAGE

WE WERE THERE... SHAY GIVEN, NEWCASTLE UNITED

It's not unusual for players to turn up a bit late for interviews – but it's very out of the ordinary for them to actually be there well ahead of time.

Shoot photographers and reporters usually aim to get to a venue well ahead of a player so they can check out potential picture locations – but when they went to see Shay Given in summer 2000 he was already there!

Then at Newcastle, the Republic of Ireland keeper was sitting in his car and waiting well before the time he had agreed to meet our team.

He posed with the No Entry sign, pulled off some saves for the camerman and even had time to joke with the painter and decorator at the Lumley Castle Hotel location – who just happened to be a big fan of rivals Sunderland!

SILVER SURFER

As fergie nears his silver anniversary with Manchester United Shoot examines his amazing Old Trafford career

When Sir Alex Ferguson left Aberdeen in 1986 he was highly coveted - spurning advances from Rangers, Arsenal and Tottenham.

The temptation to take the helm at struggling Manchester United proved too much and the Scot succeeded Ron Atkinson with the famous club languishing 21st in the old First Division.

He arrived at Old Trafford and immediately sought to address the club's drinking culture. Despite the high level of egos in the dressing room - many players soon found that it was either Fergie's way or the highway!

Ferguson quickly spelt out the major motivating factor in taking the job - knocking Liverpool off their perch! Almost 25 years later, and the two clubs sit level on the number of top tier trophies they have won - Ferguson leading the Red Devils to a remarkable haul of 11 Premier League titles.

At the end of his first season in charge, he pulled the club to a mid-table finish. They finished runners-up to Liverpool in his first full season in charge.

Two seasons of underachievement followed and Fergie was on the brink of the sack. But then came the famous Mark Robins goal that is often credited with changing the course of Ferguson's fate.

Following seven games without a win, United met the heavily favoured Nottingham Forest in the FA Cup third round. With defeat likely to secure his exit from Old Trafford, that Robins goal saved Ferguson's neck and the club went on to win the competition.

Fergie took United to a League Cup Final and Cup Winners Cup success in 1991, and he vowed the club would win the league the following season - but they fell short, 'only' winning the League Cup and Super Cup.

THE NEW DAWN...

The capture of a certain French forward kick-started a lacklustre beginning to the 1992-93 campaign, as Eric Cantona helped take the league title to Old Trafford for the first time in 26 years.

United were the first champions of the newly formed Premier League. The next season United defended their title successfully and added the FA Cup, repeating the double he achieved with Aberdeen in 1985.

Roy Keane arrived from Nottingham Forest, seen as the long-term replacement for a fading Bryan Robson. But Fergie's hunt for a third successive title fell short and the 1994-95 season was one of Fergie's most difficult.

After Cantona's now infamous kung-fu kick assault on a fan at Crystal Palace led the talismanic forward to be banned from football for eight months, United surrendered their title on the final day of the campaign - drawing with West Ham. They also lost the FA Cup Final to Everton.

THE NEW ERA...

In summer 1995, Ferguson shipped out three of his star turns - Paul Ince, Mark Hughes and Andrei Kanchelskis.

Liverpool, Newcastle and Arsenal all splashed the cash and United fell to an opening day 3-1 defeat to Aston Villa, fielding a selection of unknown youth players.

This result prompted Alan Hansen to rule United out of the title race, exclaiming: "You won't win anything with kids." Hansen, and the rest of the media, were made to eat

WHAT THEY SAY

Diego Forlan
Former United striker

"The way he treated me from the first time I arrived at Manchester was great. He was waiting for me in the stadium, took me to the hotel and showed me the facilities at the training ground. I really appreciated that. In private he is a very nice person and I have a lot of good memories of Sir Alex. He spent a lot of time with me and he taught me a lot of things."

their words as this exciting group of young players bounced back to win the league - overturning a ten-point deficit on Newcastle.

Gary Neville, his brother Phil, Nicky Butt, David Beckham and Paul Scholes came to be known as "Fergie's Fledglings". Fergie was finally put up alongside an Old Trafford great in Sir Matt Busby. And the achievements that followed would cement that comparison.

United defended their title successfully, but finished the 1998 season trophy-less as Arsene Wenger's reign at Arsenal started to bear fruit.

This prompted a £30m outlay on Dwight Yorke, Jaap Stam and Jesper Blomqvist. The season would produce Ferguson's greatest-ever achievement - an unprecedented treble, becoming the first English side to win the Champions League for 15 years and ending United's 31-year wait for the trophy.

It was the second treble Ferguson had claimed - repeating his 1983 heroics with Aberdeen - and

earned the Scot a knighthood.

In 2001, United became only the fourth side to win the English top-flight for three consecutive seasons, matching Liverpool's record set in 1991 of ten successive top-two finishes. Fergie was certainly knocking the Merseyside club off their perch...

BORN AGAIN...

The next season was supposed to be Fergie's last after a public announcement of retirement - but he agreed to stay on for another season - splashing out £30m on Rio Ferdinand.

Trailing Arsenal by eight points with two months of the campaign remaining, United won ten and drew one of their 11 remaining games as they overturned the Londoners - leading Ferguson to describe it as his most satisfying title success.

A three-year barren spell in the league followed. With young players such as Cristiano Ronaldo and Wayne Rooney, unknown quantities in Patrice Evra and Nemanja Vidic and more established players such as Michael Carrick, Edwin Van der Sar and Park Ji-Sung arriving, Ferguson was

WHAT THEY SAY

Cristiano Ronaldo
The star he sold for £80m

"Ferguson is a maestro. For me he was my father in football. He was crucial in my career and, outside football, was a great human being with me. Talent isn't everything. You can have it from the cradle, but it is necessary to learn the trade to be the best. I spent six years at United and I owe them everything that I am today."

WHAT THEY SAY

Jamie Carragher
Stalwart of rivals Liverpool

"I've got more respect for Alex Ferguson than anyone else in the game. Managers who have been going for a long time like Ferguson come under pressure to produce winning sides even when they've lost top players and they always come up with the answers."

quietly building a fearsome team.

To mark Ferguson's 20-year anniversary with the club, these players won their first league title in four years, prompting a run of three straight Championships.

The team also claimed United's third Champions League success in 2008, seeing off Chelsea on penalties. League Cup victories were added in 2009 and 2010, while Barcelona denied United successive Champions League glory in 2009.

Knowing that one more league title would achieve what he had set out to do at the start of his reign - overhaul Liverpool - Fergie was determined to claim the 2010 title but lost out to Chelsea.

Ferguson is still determined to put United above Liverpool in terms of league titles won...

FERGIE'S BEST SIGNINGS

➔ SIR ALEX FERGUSONS MANCHESTER UNITED ACHIEVEMENTS

PREMIER LEAGUE:
1993, 1994, 1996, 1997, 1999, 2000, 2001, 2003, 2007, 2008, 2009

FA CUP:
1990, 1994, 1996, 1999, 2004

FOOTBALL LEAGUE CUP:
1992, 2006, 2009, 2010

COMMUNITY SHIELD:
1990, 1993, 1994, 1996, 1997, 2003, 2007,

UEFA CHAMPIONS LEAGUE:
1999, 2008

UEFA CUP WINNERS CUP: 1991

UEFA SUPER CUP: 1991

INTERCONTINENTAL CUP: 1999

FIFA CLUB WORLD CUP: 2008

PREMIER LEAGUE MANAGER OF THE YEAR:
1994, 1996, 1997, 1999, 2000, 2003, 2007, 2008, 2009

➔ ERIC CANTONA

A £1.2m signing from Leeds, Cantona inspired United to their first Premier League title, going on to claim four titles in five seasons including two doubles, and becoming a club legend in the process.

➔ PETER SCHMEICHEL

His £530,000 move to United in 1991 was described by Sir Alex a decade later as 'the bargain of the century'. One of the greatest keepers of all time, Schmeichel won everything there was to win with United - his final game coming in the 1999 Champions League Final and sealing the treble. What a way to sign off!

➔ ANDY COLE

Signed for a then British record £7m in 1995, striker Cole became a key component in one of United's most successful teams of all time. His role in the treble-winning season cannot be underestimated - though his partnership with Dwight Yorke is rightly lauded, he finished as club top scorer that season.

➔ NEMANJA VIDIC

The Serbia defender arrived for £7m in 2006 as a virtual unknown and has gone on to become one of the finest defenders in the world. His arrival was part of Ferguson's reinvention of United, as they ended three title-less years with three successive championships, a Champions League title and two League Cups.

➔ EDWIN VAN DER SAR

Another key part of that team, Van der Sar has offered a reliable and quality pair of hands in goal for the first time since Schmeichel. His £2m transfer fee has easily been paid back since his move in 2005 from Fulham.

Aberdeen boss Alex Ferguson (inset) is in no hurry to part company with his talented centre-back Alex McLeish (No. 5).

NO SALE AT ABERDEEN
hopes firebrand Fergie

"We must look to the new season," says Fergie. "Europe is vital to this club and we will have to make sure of a place in this arena.

"Possibly I expected too much of my younger players this time around, but the experience will not have done them any harm.

"John Hewitt, Neil Simson, Ian Angus, Dougie Bell, Andy Watson and the others will all be better players after this season.

"There is still an abundance of talent here. No-one should count us out now . . . that would be foolish."

The unfortunate avalanche of injuries left Aberdeen short in vital areas in the team, but Fergie has been in no rush to part with huge sums of money to patch up his team. The Archibald cash is largely untouched, although he did part with £80,000 to Luton for striker Andy Harrow.

He has already made it clear he will not be held to ransom and he will not be involved in an auction for a player. He made what he considered a fair bid for Airdrie goalgetter Sandy Clark — around £150,000 — earlier this year and was told to add to it.

Fergie refused, saying: "I'm not paying over my evaluation of a player. Some of the prices being asked these days are ridiculous."

Aberdeen, then, are disappointed at the way things have gone for them this season . . . a season that promised so much back in August, but has failed to yield a rich harvest.

Alex Ferguson and his players are already gearing themselves for next season. Stand by once more for the invasion of the Red Army!

ABERDEEN manager Alex Ferguson has a chair in his office at Pittodrie which he called his 'Steve Archibald Seat'.

That's where Archibald used to sit and talk things over with The Dons boss before the international striker moved across the border for almost £1 million to Spurs.

Fergie did everything in his power to keep Archibald at Aberdeen and he is just as determined to hold to any other player he thinks can do a good job for his first team.

"Transfer talks only serve to unsettle a player," says Fergie. "I should know . . . I played for enough clubs myself, didn't I?"

The Dons supremo, once a feared striker, started his career with Queen's Park before moving on to St Johnstone, Dunfermline, Rangers, Falkirk and Ayr United. As a manager he has been charge of East Stirling and St Mirren before settling at Aberdeen.

Adamant

Now, after the relative failure of this season, Fergie is looking to the future — and he is adamant that club will resist any offers they might get for Alex McLeish, Gordon Strachan or anyone else he feels should stay at Pittodrie.

Last season, firebrand Fergie admitted: "It was great to win the Premier Division Championship, but as we won't retain it the pressure will be on us all the way to do better next season. Let's see how we cope. I want us to do things in style. I think that is very important."

The decline of Aberdeen by their own high standards can be put down to many reasons. Archibald's goal power has been sorely missed although, at one stage, Mark McGhee seemed to have the answer.

Midfielder John McMaster's season was cruelly cut short with a leg injury. Stewart Kennedy, the international right-back, was the next to drop out of the team through injury and, of course, midfield mastermind Gordon Strachan was missed during his lengthy, enforced absence.

Aberdeen, though, battled on and still managed to take six out of a possible eight points from Celtic in the League, and that is no mean feat considering the way the Parkhead men have been performing in recent months.

Mark McGhee promised to replace the goalscoring talents of Steve Archibald for Aberdeen earlier this season.

CLASSIC IMAGE

BECKHAM'S BACK 2001

David Beckham lives a fairytale life – but the script couldn't have been better written for this World Cup 2002 qualifier at Old Trafford in October 2001. Deep into injury time England trailed Greece 2-1 and only local hero Becks looked like saving the day. He'd already missed with five long-rang free-kicks when he stepped up yet again for a kick... and crashed home the equaliser with seconds remaining. England were through to the World Cup finals in South Korea and Japan!

A player that has flown under the radar for some time, but whose star has always shone brightly in Holland, Demebele's arrival at Craven Cottage probably prompted a blank response or two.

Who was this player new boss Mark Hughes had splashed out £5m on?

The 23-year-old had already established himself in Holland – for the past five seasons his stock has been on a gradual ascent, with a Premier League move the inevitable ending.

After signing from Germinal Beerschot, Demebele top-scored for struggling Willem II, catching the attention of AZ Alkmaar in the summer of 2006.

That season he was a crucial part of the side that almost won a surprise title – Louis van Gaal's men were only pipped by PSV on the final day of the season.

After a disappointing 2007-08 campaign, Dembele and AZ bounced back, claiming the Eredivisie title, with the Belgium forward the side's star turn.

That season they also won the Dutch Cup to complete a memorable Double.

Despite not repeating that form last season, Dembele was wanted by various Premier League clubs, with Birmingham's Alex McLeish even stating at one point that he believed a deal was close for the forward.

Hughes pounced quickly to land his man – a relatively young player who can be deployed up top, on the flanks or 'in the hole' as a playmaker.

Dembele is two-footed, quick and dangerous when floating in-field from the left wing. An exciting prospect for Fulham fans.

WHAT THEY SAY: "I'm glad we have finalised the deal with Moussa Dembele. It is important we add strength and depth to enable us to compete. Moussa is strong and quick and will add another dimension to our attacking options."
Mark Hughes, Fulham manager

A new lease of life
EURO HITMAN

ⓘ FACT FILE

MOUSSA DEMBÉLÉ

POSITION:	Forward/Winger
BIRTH PLACE:	Wilrijk, Belgium
BIRTH DATE:	July 16, 1987
HEIGHT:	1.85m (6ft 1in)
CLUBS:	Germinal Beerschot, Willem II, AZ, Fulham
INTERNATIONAL:	Belgium

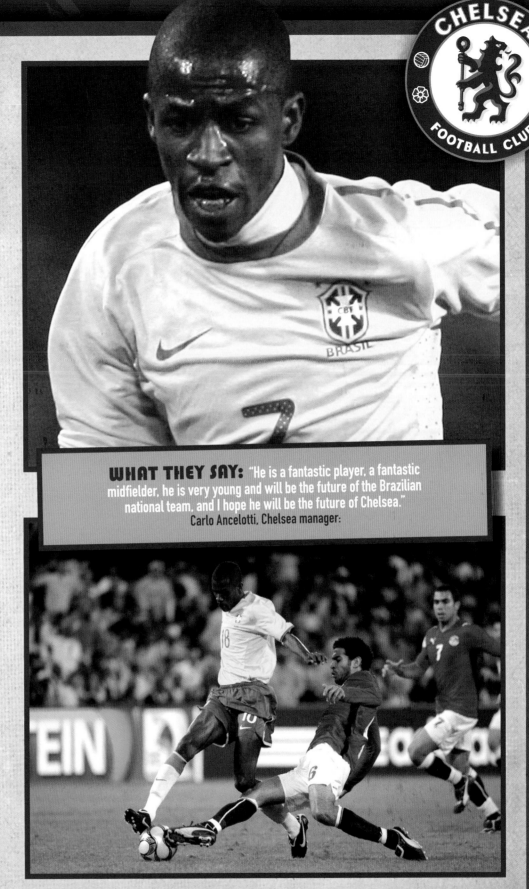

FACT FILE

RAMIRES

POSITION:	Midfielder
BIRTH PLACE:	Rio de Janeiro, Brazil
BIRTH DATE:	March 24, 1987
HEIGHT:	1.80m (5ft 11in)
CLUBS:	Joinville, Cruzeiro, Benfica, Chelsea
INTERNATIONAL:	Brazil

Benfica's Double-winning side from season 2009-10 is slowly but surely being broken up and distributed amongst Europe's big boys.

The Portuguese club's success drew admiring glances for a host of their stars. Having ended a five-year wait for a league title, it was inevitable that the nucleus of that side would move on.

Star man Angel di Maria went to Real Madrid, before Ramires followed him out of the exit door – Chelsea his destination.

The £17m deal secures the Blues a player who should rejuvenate their midfield area. Having released the likes of Michael Ballack, Deco, Joe Cole and Juliano Belletti, Ramires was expected to alter the dynamics of the Chelsea midfield.

Such is his energy he was dubbed 'the Blue Kenyan' by Cruzeiro fans during his time there – after the club's colours (blue) and his athlete-like engine.

Carlo Ancelotti also praised the dynamic midfielder's versatility. The player can be used in the anchor role of Chelsea's diamond, or on the right-hand side.

Part of the Brazil side that won the 2009 Confederations Cup, Ramires impressed again for Brazil in South Africa – his sublime pass setting up Robinho in the 3-0 defeat of Chile.

His absence was obvious when suspension ruled him out of Brazil's quarter-finals defeat to Holland, the side lacking the same rhythm and style that had been present when Ramires was involved.

Having spent just one season in Europe with Benfica, Ramires was hoping to continue the success he tasted with the Portuguese champions at Chelsea.

"Every player in the world would love to play for Chelsea and it's a great opportunity that was given to me," he said. "I will give my best to repay this chance, and I am very happy."

WHAT THEY SAY: "He is a fantastic player, a fantastic midfielder, he is very young and will be the future of the Brazilian national team, and I hope he will be the future of Chelsea."
Carlo Ancelotti, Chelsea manager:

A new lease of life
SAMBA STAR

It would have been easy to write off Richard Dunne's career once he left mega-rich Manchester City for Aston Villa for £5m in August 2009.

But anyone who thought he was on the way down would have been totally wrong. You never doubt this giant central-defender.

Dunne began his career at Everton but it was after his move to Man City in 2000 that he really pushed himself to the fore and became a regular for the Republic of Ireland in the process.

During his time at Maine Road and Eastlands, Dunne was City's Player of the Year on a record-busting FOUR occasions. He was also Ireland's Player of the Year in 2008.

His sheer consistency and dedication – even sticking with City when they were relegated during his first season – earned him total respect from the fans.

But the arrival of big money buys Kolo Toure and Joleon Lescott saw his rather unceremonious departure. Villa boss Martin O'Neill was smart enough to know that even at £5m Dunne was going to be a good signing and was quickly in with a contract.

With 44 appearances in his first season, it was money well spent. Dunne's Villa career continued in the same vein as his City one had ended with consistency and earned him a place in the PFA Team of the Year for 2009-10.

The Ireland defender was denied a place at last summer's World Cup by Thierry Henry's infamous handball goal, but he remains a key figure for both club and country.

An ever-present during the World Cup qualifying campaign, Dunne will be hoping for retribution as Ireland begin qualification for Euro 2012.

WHAT THEY SAY: "He has been immense for us. I am absolutely delighted with him. We obviously got a bit of luck with what was happening at Manchester City at the time. But for £5m he has been incredible value."
Martin O'Neill , former Aston Villa Manager

A new lease of life
DUNNE DEAL

ⓘ FACT FILE

RICHARD PATRICK DUNNE

POSITION:	Defender
BIRTH PLACE:	Dublin
BIRTH DATE:	September 21, 1979
HEIGHT:	1.88m (6ft 2in)
CLUBS:	Everton, Manchester City, Aston Villa
INTERNATIONAL:	Republic of Ireland

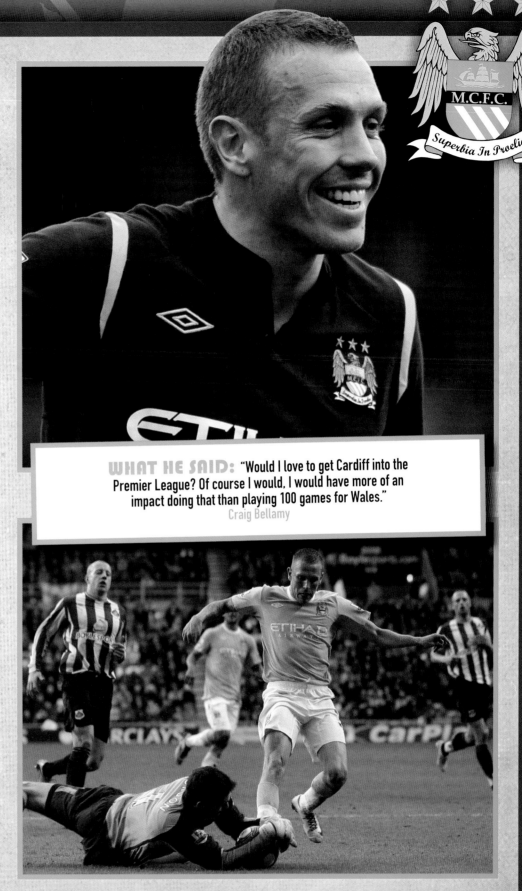

Craig Bellamy can breathe fire into a game with his livewire performances. He's often criticised, often shouts off his own mouth but nearly always finds the back of the net when it matters.

But just as important is his dedication to the game, his battling qualities and the skill that has created chances for his team-mates.

Bellars is just as fiery as the legendary dragons that give his Wales side its nickname. That enthusiastic approach has often got him into trouble with officials and fellow players but there is no doubting it's a vital part of his game.

Despite a series of injuries he's still got speed and he can turn defenders inside out or jink past them, leaving them totally stranded.

He's said he wont ever give up on playing for Wales – and there has never been any shortage of clubs willing to take a risk and sign him.

Man City fan Noel Gallagher, of rock group Oasis, described the £14m his side paid for Bellamy as "insane". But surely even he now has to admit that the little guy made a big contribution to the Eastlands side.

While City's influx of mega-money foreign stars stole the headlines, Bellamy's graft and determination established him as a key part of the City side that came so close to grabbing fourth in 2009-10.

Despite those impressive performances, City's spending meant that the forward wouldn't be registered in their 25-man Premier League squad.

Eager to play football, Bellamy completed a fairytale season-long loan move to home-town club Cardiff for 2010-11.

WHAT HE SAID: "Would I love to get Cardiff into the Premier League? Of course I would, I would have more of an impact doing that than playing 100 games for Wales."
Craig Bellamy

A new lease of life
DRAGON KING

Last Team Tottenham

At £10m Darren Bent didn't arrive at Sunderland on the cheap – but he certainly proved to be worth the cash with a deluge of goals.

Those goals made him the highest-scoring Englishman in the 2009-10 Premier League and ensured the Black Cats stayed in the top-flight.

Sunderland boss Steve Bruce has a pretty good track record in buying players and Bent can be added to that list.

Bent was a hit during his time at Ipswich, where he started his career as a trainee, and that earned him a £2.5m move to Charlton.

His goals record at the Valley was almost one every other game and led to Tottenham forking out a club record £16.5m for the hitman.

Despite scoring goals at White Hart Lane it wasn't the best time of his career. He wasn't always first-choice and there were signs that he wasn't the most popular player with the management team.

He scored on his Sunderland debut in August 2009 to give them victory over Bolton and 25 goals in 40 games made him the club's top scorer at the end of the season.

All but one of those goals came in the Premier League but they weren't enough to earn the fast, skilled marksman a place in England's 2010 World Cup squad.

After England's lack of potency in South Africa, another goal-laden campaign could propel him into international contention once again

WHAT HE SAID: "My football has done the talking. I was miserable at Tottenham because I wasn't playing. I have become a stronger person and I can't do much more except keep on scoring." Darren Bent

ⓘ FACT FILE

DARREN ASHLEY BENT

POSITION:	Striker
BIRTH PLACE:	Tooting, South London
BIRTH DATE:	February 6, 1984
HEIGHT:	1.8m (5ft 11in)
CLUBS:	Ipswich, Charlton, Tottenham, Sunderland
INTERNATIONAL:	England

A new lease of life
DAZZLER DARREN

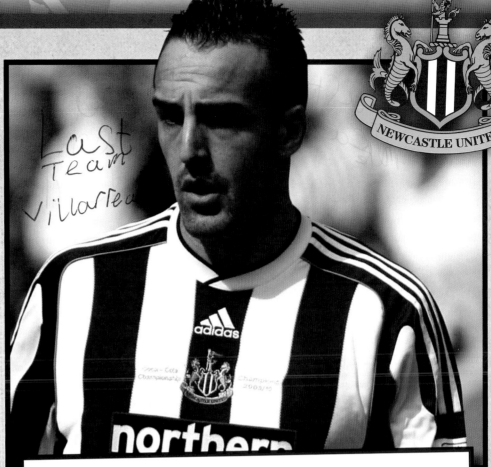

There's more than one Jose who is a bit special – as defender Jose Enrique has proved to Newcastle United fans.

There were high hopes when the Spanish left-back arrived at St. James' Park from Villarreal in August 2007.

Then-boss Sam Allardyce sang the praises of his £6m signing but the fans were puzzled why the defender wasn't give more chances to prove his worth.

Allardyce suggested the player needed to adapt and that he was young and needed more experience, yet when he was given his chance Enrique nearly always proved his worth.

Enrique's second season saw him as a virtual regular for the first-team but the campaign ended in relegation.

Newcastle's fall to the Championship could easily have led to Enrique's departure from Tyneside with clubs in his home country expressing interest, and suggestions that Chelsea had watched him.

But by now the player was an adopted Geordie and expressed his desire not only to help the side regain Premier League status, but to stay with them for a long time.

Supporters saw the true form of the hard-tackling, fast running and raiding full-back and the results were a new chant from the terraces of "Jose, Jose, Jose, Jose..."

Geordie fans also voted for him as their Player of the Year, the ultimate accolade.

WHAT HE SAID: *"I worry for my team – I love the city, I love the club and I don't care about signing for another team."* Jose Enrique

A new lease of life
FANS SING ENRIQUE'S PRAISES

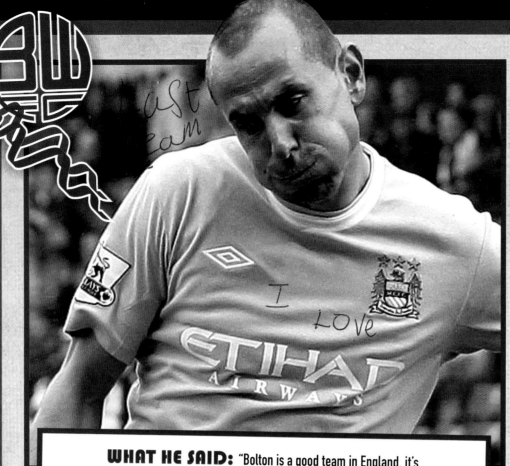

WHAT HE SAID: "Bolton is a good team in England, it's not one of the big names but I came here because I spoke with the manager and he told me he wants to play football, to play with wingers and to score more goals — that's very important for me."
Martin Petrov

A new lease of life
CITY OUTCAST

An explosive left winger, Manchester City fans were denied the privilege of seeing Martin Petrov at his best for much of his three-year spell at Eastlands.

His debut campaign for the Blues was scintillating, but injury ravaged his next two seasons, dropping him down the pecking order as City continued to spend big.

With his contract up, it was clear that Roberto Mancini wouldn't be making an offer to keep the Bulgaria midfielder at the City of Manchester stadium.

A host of clubs were linked, but it was Bolton who snared the former Wolfsburg and Atletico Madrid wideman.

Trotters boss Owen Coyle has already expressed his excitement at the capture, describing Petrov as "probably one of the best Bosman transfers available".

With the former Burnley coach looking to instigate a change in style at the Reebok, altering the 'kick and rush' policy previously adopted to something a bit more continental, Petrov will offer a genuine threat from wide positions.

Coyle will be hoping that Petrov can regain the form that prompted Atletico to splash out £8m to sign him.

A title-winner in Bulgaria with CSKA Sofia and Switzerland with Servette FC, Petrov will be part of Coyle's revolution in Lancashire – charged with propelling the side into contention for a European spot.

With a point to prove after his injury-disrupted time at Eastlands, Petrov may be just the man to do that for the Whites.

(i) FACT FILE

MARTIN PETYOV PETROV

POSITION:	Winger
BIRTH PLACE:	Vratsa, Bulgaria
BIRTH DATE:	January 15, 1979
HEIGHT:	1.80m (5ft 11in)
CLUBS:	Botev Vratsa, CSKA Sofia, Serveette, Wolfsburg, Manchester City, Bolton
INTERNATIONAL:	Bulgaria

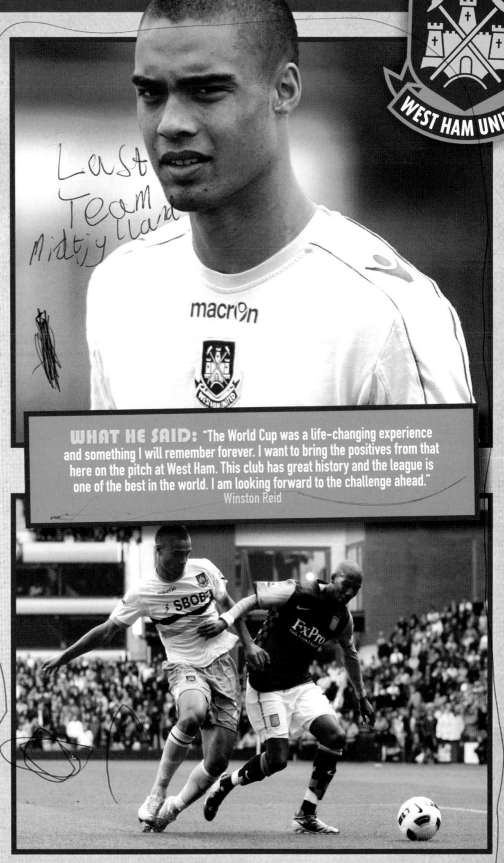

Whatever happens now in his career, Winston Reid will forever be immortalised in New Zealand folklore.

His last-gasp equaliser against Slovakia in the World Cup secured his country's first-ever point in a finals match.

It completed the most romantic of stories. Based in Denmark, Reid had never registered on the international radar and was included in the New Zealand World Cup squad despite the fact that manager Ricki Herbert had never seen him play.

The risk paid off incredibly, as Reid shone in the Kiwis' three draws – including a 1-1 tie with reigning World Champions Italy. Remarkably, the Kiwis were the only side to remain unbeaten during South Africa 2010.

Reid's performances brought him to the attention of various European scouts, who will have noted with glee the fact that he graduated from the same youth academy as Simon Kjaer, the highly touted defender who joined Wolfsburg from Palermo last summer.

The 22-year-old's £4m switch to West Ham would've been unfathomable prior to the World Cup, such is the extent of his meteoric rise during a whirlwind summer.

Capable of playing as a centre back, he was expected to feature most at right back, the position in which he was deployed for the All Whites and where he caught Avram Grant's eye.

After five seasons in the FC Midtjylland first-team, Reid will now look to establish himself at the top of English football.

WEST HAM UNITED

WHAT HE SAID: "The World Cup was a life-changing experience and something I will remember forever. I want to bring the positives from that here on the pitch at West Ham. This club has great history and the league is one of the best in the world. I am looking forward to the challenge ahead."
Winston Reid

A new lease of life
KIWI HERO

113

It's funny how chance encounters can influence the future.

When Roy Hodgson signed a then 20-year-old Christian Poulsen for Copenhagen in 2000, few would expect that the duo would be pairing up at Liverpool ten years later.

The pair led the Danish club to the league title that season, before Hodgson departed for Udinese.

Poulsen remained with the club to lead them to a successful defence of their championship, before moving to German giants Schalke.

The deal, approximately £6m, was the record sale by a Danish club at that time.

An attacking player before the switch, Poulsen started off as right back for Schalke, before eventually cementing himself as a holding midfielder.

When his contract expired in 2006, he ignored advances from the Milan duo Inter and AC, opting instead to join Sevilla – helping them to a UEFA Cup and Spanish Cup Double.

Italy, though, was always in the background of Poulsen's career. Eventually he made the switch to Serie A, joining Juventus in an £8m deal.

A first-team regular for the Old Lady, his availability in summer 2010 was a surprise to many – particularly the reduced price tag placed on his head.

With uncertainty surrounding Javier Mascherano's future and the general lack of depth in Liverpool's midfield, Hodgson moved swiftly to arrange a reunion with his former charge in Merseyside.

At just £4.5m, he could prove to be an absolute steal.

WHAT THEY SAY: "Christian is an all-round player. He is capable of scoring goals, a good passer of the ball and a good defender too. I don't see him being limited to one particular role. "For me, it was a very simple decision when I heard he might be available at what we considered to be a very reasonable price. We need as many good players as we can get and if you let these opportunities pass you by, sometimes you can regret it."
Roy Hodgson, Liverpool manager

A new lease of life
GREAT DANE

ⓘ FACT FILE

CHRISTIAN BAGER POULSEN

POSITION:	Holding midfielder
BIRTH PLACE:	Asnæs, Denmark
BIRTH DATE:	February 28, 1980
HEIGHT:	1.83m (6ft 0in)
CLUBS:	Holbæk, Copenhagen, Schalke 04, Sevilla, Juventus, Liverpool
INTERNATIONAL:	Denmark

PARTING SHOT

PLAYER FILE
Your guide to the stars and their lifestyles...

THIS MONTH: KEVIN DOYLE READING STRIKER

NAME: Kevin Doyle.
NICKNAME: Doyley.
BIRTHPLACE: Adamstown, Eire, September 18, 1983.
MARRIED: Girlfriend.
PREVIOUS CLUBS: Cork City.
CAR: Six-Series BMW.
MOBILE PHONE: Sony Eriksson A800.

FOOTBALL

BEST MOMENT IN FOOTBALL?
"The whole of last season, playing and scoring goals for Reading, making my Ireland debut and then picking up The Championship title at the end of the campaign. It was a great year for me and I never expected it to go half as well as it did."

WORST MOMENT IN FOOTBALL?
"Being hauled off after 55 minutes playing for Ireland Under-21s against Switzerland. I was up against Philippe Senderos and had an absolute stinker - thankfully the highs have outweighed the lows so far."

THE BEST PLAYER YOU HAVE FACED?
"Probably Senderos in that match! He was not that well known at the time but has gone on to establish himself as one of the best defenders in the Premiership. I am sure I will face a few more this like him this season."

HAS THE BOSS EVER GIVEN YOU A TICKING OFF?
"I have never had one off Steve Coppell but I used to think Pat Dolan, my manager at Cork City, was bullying me. He used to slaughter me after every game and there were a couple of occasions when he kicked tables across the room. I also got a few Lucozade bottles hurled in my direction. He's since told me he just wanted me to fulfil my potential."

YOU'RE ALLOWED TO SIGN ANY PLAYED IN THE WORLD FOR YOUR TEAM. WHO WOULD YOU BUY?
"Thierry Henry. He is a striker, he scores goals, he creates goals and has fantastic skill. He is a class act."

ANY SUPERSTITIONS?
"I do not believe in leprechauns, if that's what you think. A lot of my mates are really superstitious but I just let nature take its course.

LIFESTYLE

THE MOST FAMOUS PERSON YOU HAVE EVER MET?
"Probably "Big Phil" Scolari. He presented me with Player of the Tournament after an Under-21 competition in Portugal. It's not every day you meat a World Cup-winning manager."

FAVOURITE TV PROGRAMME?
"I'm a bit of a girl when it comes to television. I love Coronation Street and my girlfriend has got me well into Love Island. I hate Big Brother but am a big fan of Friends – for the women."

WHO IS IN CHARGE OF THE CLUB STEREO AND WHAT DOES HE PLAY?
"Ibrahima Sonko. He appointed himself to the role and he is too big for anyone to argue but the stuff he plays is terrible, too loud. Most of the time I am grateful when the gaffer switches it off to give a team talk."

LAST CD YOU BOUGHT?
"Jack Johnson's album In Between Dreams. My girlfriend Jennifer got me into him and now I play it all the time. It is very chilled-out and relaxed and helps me to wind down after games."

WHAT MUSIC IS IN YOUR CAR AT THE MOMENT?
"I tend to listen to the radio rather than CDs when I'm driving. I love listening to Magic. They play a lot of cheese and all the old classics."

FAVOURITE MEAL?
"When I am not playing I always treat myself to a piece of steak (cooked medium rare), chips, mushrooms and onions - but don't tell the boss."

WORST DRESSED TEAM-MATE?
"Stephen Hunt. My fellow Irishman has shocking taste in clothes. When it's really hot he parades round in a pair of white cotton trousers and takes a load of stick."

LAST BOOK YOU READ?
"I am reading a biography on John F. Kennedy. I have always been interested in American politics and the events leading up to his

YOU ARE OFFERED THOUSANDS OF POUNDS TO WRITE A WARTS-AND-ALL AUTOBIOGRAPHY, WOULD YOU DO IT?
"Definitely not. I hate reading football autobiographies and cannot think why anyone buys them. You are never going to paint yourself in a negative life so it is a pointless exercise. I'd rather be poor."

assassination. I recently read the Da Vinci Code and that is good."

LAST FILM YOU SAW?
"The new Superman movie. It was okay but the battle at the end was a bit disappointing – it was too easy for him. 6.5 out of ten."

WHAT WOULD YOU BE IF NOT A FOOTBALLER?
"Probably pulling pints in my mum and dad's pub back in Ireland. I worked there right up until I came to England and loved it."

TAKE YOUR PICK...

PREMIERSHIP OR CHAMPIONS LEAGUE?
"Champions League (I love the music before matches)."

MOTD OR SKY SPORTS?
"MOTD."

IPOD OR PLAYSTATION?
"ipod."

GUINESS OR LAGER
"Guinness."

CRICKET OR RUGBY
"Rugby (but I prefer hurling)."

Doyle cost Reading just £78,00, before moving on to Wolves for £6.5m

PARTING SHOT

PLAYER FILE
Your guide to the stars and their lifestyles...

THIS MONTH: PAUL KONCHESKY WEST HAM UNITED DEFENDER

NAME: Paul Konchesky.
NICKNAME: Konch.
BIRTHPLACE: Barking, Essex, May 15, 1981.
PREVIOUS CLUBS: Charlton, Tottenham (loan).
CAR: Range Rover Sport.
MOBILE PHONE: Nokia N73.

FOOTBALL

BEST MOMENT IN FOOTBALL?
"Both of my England caps. To make my international debut at Upton Park against Australia is a moment I'll savour for the rest of my life and then, more recently, to play against a team of Argentina's calibre was a wonderful experience. Hopefully there will be more caps to come."

AND YOUR WORST?

"Probably the recent poor run that West Ham have been on, especially the Carling Cup defeat at Chesterfield. People are saying it's down to the Argentinian players and the take-over talk, but we were losing games before all that happened. We've got to snap out of it and fast."

BEST PLAYER YOU'VE FACED?
"Cristiano Ronaldo. He's a few years younger than me but I remember coming up against him when I played for England Under-21s – which tells you how highly he was rated in Portugal. He's tall, strong, is full of tricks and has incredibly quick feet."

HAS THE BOSS EVER GIVEN YOU A TICKING OFF?

"Not at West Ham, but I remember Curbs [Alan Curbishley] having a go at me when I was sent-off for Charlton reserves against West Ham. I got a three-game ban for swearing at a referee."

YOU'RE ALLOWED TO SIGN ANY PLAYER IN THE WORLD FOR YOUR TEAM…
"I'd probably buy a whole new team the way we've been playing lately!

"Seriously, it would have to be either Steven Gerrard or Thierry Henry as they have everything. If I had to choose one it'd be Thierry because he scores more goals."

ANY SUPERSTITIONS?
"I always put my right sock on before my left, my right boot before my left… but it's still nowhere near as bad as Anton Ferdinand's pre-match routine. No, I won't tell you, you'll have to ask him sometime."

LIFESTYLE

FAVOURITE TV PROGRAMME?
"It would probably be Only Fools and Horses, although I must say I've got into X Factor and Ant and Dec's Saturday Night Takeaway after a home game."

THE MOST FAMOUS PERSON YOU HAVE EVER MET?
"I come up against famous footballers every week, so it'd be one of them. Take your pick: Rooney, Giggs, Henry, Terry…"

WHO IS IN CHARGE OF THE CLUB STEREO AND WHAT DOES HE PLAY?
"Marlon Harewood and Nigel Reo-Coker are in charge and they'll have some R&B or Hip-Hop on. It's usually a mix CD one

DILEMMA QUESTIONS

THERE'S JUST 15 MINUTES OF THE CUP FINAL GONE AND A SHOT IS GOAL-BOUND BUT OUT OF REACH. DO YOU TRY AND HEAD IT OR PUSH IT AWAY WITH A HAND?
"I think it's instinctive that you'll use your hand. I know it'll leave the team with ten men, but you'll possibly be saving a goal and sometimes ten men do well against 11."

of them has put together."

LAST CD YOU BOUGHT?
"Lionel Richie's Greatest Hits! I bought it a few years back but it went missing – I can only assume one of the lads took it – so I had to buy a replacement the other day. Lionel's a ledge!"

WHAT MUSIC IS IN YOUR CAR AT THE MOMENT?
"One of Marlon's mix CDs. I'll usually listen to R&B, but on the way to games I'll probably play some garage to get myself pumped up for the match."

FAVOURITE MEAL?
"Chinese. I'm not into one particular dish, I like the full monty. When I go down to my local take-away, I just ask for the usual, and they know how to sort me out!"

TAKE YOUR PICK…

SOCCER AM OR MOTD?
"Soccer AM."

IPOD OR PLAYSTATION?
"PlayStation."

TRAINERS OR SHOES?
"Trainers."

BLONDES OR BRUNETTES?
"Blondes."

PARTING SHOT

PLAYER FILE

Your guide to the stars and their lifestyles...

THIS MONTH: JIMMY BULLARD, WIGAN ATHLETIC MIDFIELDER

NAME: James Richard Bullard.
NICKNAME: Bulldog.
BIRTHPLACE: Newham, East London, October 23, 1978.
MARRIED: Girlfriend.
CAR: Range Rover.
MOBILE PHONE: Nokia.

FOOTBALL

BEST MOMENT IN FOOTBALL?
"Getting promoted last year. I had an idea we had a great chance but to actually do it was class."

AND THE WORST?
"I've not had many touch wood. Having to leave West Ham after four years was hard, but I admit it was probably time to go."

HAS THE BOSS EVER GIVEN YOU A TICKING OFF?
"Every week!"

YOU'RE ALLOWED TO SIGN ANY PLAYER IN THE WORLD FOR YOUR TEAM. WHO WOULD YOU BUY?
"Ronaldhino or Robinho."

WHAT'S THE BIGGEST WIND-UP YOU'VE BEEN A VICTIM OF?
"My team-mates Alan Mahon and Leighton Baines put a bucket of water outside my hotel room so I got a right soaking when I opened the door."

THE BEST PLAYER YOU

HAVE FACED?
"That's a tough one, probably Joe Cole or Steven Gerrard (below)."

ANY SUPERSTITIONS?
"In the line up coming out of the tunnel I have to be in front of a left midfielder. I know… that's a very bad one."

LIFESTYLE

MOST FAMOUS PERSON YOU'VE MET?
"Stu Conroy, he fishes for England and has bronze and gold medals in the World Angling Championships. He's my hero."

FAVOURITE TV PROGRAMME?
"EastEnders."

WHO IS IN CHARGE OF THE CLUB STEREO AND WHAT DOES HE PLAY?
"Jason Roberts who plays rap and R and B and Leighton Baines who puts on mostly Indie. They're both rubbish."

THE LAST CD YOU BOUGHT?
"Robbie Williams, Intensive Care."

WHAT MUSIC IS IN YOUR CAR AT THE MOMENT?
"UB40, Robbie Williams and U2."

FAVOURITE DESIGNER?
"Anything that is me. If I like it I wear it."

WORST DRESSED TEAM-MATE?
"The new boy Paul Scharner has some bad clothes. Pascal (Chimbonda) is bad too."

LAST BOOK YOU READ?
"Don't really read books,

magazines…. fishing ones."

IF NOT A FOOTBALLER WHAT WOULD YOU BE?
"A professional angler or golfer."

IF MONEY WERE NO OBJECT WHAT CAR WOULD YOU BUY?
"A Bentley, smart."

DILEMMA QUESTIONS

YOUR SIDE GET A LATE PENALTY AND YOU NEED A GOAL TO WIN A BET WITH A MATE. DO YOU GRAB THE BALL, ALTHOUGH YOU'RE NOT THE REGULAR TAKER?
"Yes, definitely."

AN OPPONENT IS DOWN INJURED BUT YOU HAVE THE CHANCE TO SCORE. DO YOU SHOOT OR KICK THE BALL INTO TOUCH?
"Shoot for goal, unless it's a really bad injury."

TAKE YOUR PICK…

REAL MADRID OR BARCELONA?
"Real Madrid."

BEER OR WINE?
"Wine."

MOTD OR SKY SPORTS?
"Match of the Day"

CRICKET OR RUGBY?
"Rugby."

IPOD OR PLAYSTATION?
"iPod."

JENNIFER ANISTON OR BRITNEY SPEARS?
"Jennifer Aniston"

PARTING SHOT

PLAYER FILE

Your guide to the stars and their lifestyles...

THIS MONTH: STEVEN TAYLOR, NEWCASTLE DEFENDER

NAME: Steven Taylor
NICKNAME: Tayls
BIRTHPLACE: Greenwich, January 23, 1986.
PREVIOUS CLUBS: Newcastle (from trainee), Wycombe (loan).
MARITAL STATUS: Single.
CAR: BMW X5
MOBILE PHONE: Vertu

FOOTBALL

BEST MOMENT IN FOOTBALL?
"Making my full debut in front of 52,000 Geordies at St. James' Park against Everton in 2004. It was a boyhood ambition achieved, like it is for every lad that's ever been a Newcastle fan. It was hard to take it all in at the time because I had a job to do, but on reflection it was just a wonderful moment."

...AND YOUR WORST?
"Getting sent off in front of the same 52,000 fans against Aston Villa. People might remember the game – it's the one where I went down like I'd been shot and I'm not particularly proud of it. I got a lot of stick off my friends

when they saw it on TV, but you learn from these things."

BEST PLAYER YOU'VE FACED?
"Ruud van Nistelrooy's goal record says it all. His movement is fantastic and if you give him half a chance he will punish you. He is so clever that it feels like he's marking you, not you marking him, and he plays off your shoulder which makes it even more difficult."

HAS THE BOSS EVERY GIVEN YOU A TICKING OFF?
"I'm always getting ticked off, even in training, and it can be from my fellow players, not just the boss! But you take these things on the chin and take what's being said on board, because you can never stop learning. Fortunately for me, our boss Glenn Roeder was a defender himself, so I'm learning a great deal."

YOU'RE ALLOWED TO SIGN ANY PLAYER IN THE WORLD FOR YOUR TEAM...
"John Terry. I was fortunate

enough to meet him and have a chat with him when we played Chelsea at St. James' Park a couple of seasons ago. He gave me a signed shirt, which takes pride of place in my house, He inspires me to one day follow in his footsteps to the England senior team."

ANY SUPERSTITIONS?
"I always wear two pairs of socks in the warm-up, and one of them will be inside out. I do this to stop me getting blisters."

LIFESTYLE

THE MOST FAMOUS PERSON YOU HAVE MET?
"I can't honestly say I have ever met any celebrities. I suppose the closest would be Alan Shearer but he's not a celebrity – he's a legend!"

FAVOURITE TV PROGRAMME?
"X-Factor. Leona was the best from the last series and I'll always catch it on a Saturday night if we've had a home game. The TV is always on in my house and if I'm not watching the box I'll get a few of the lads round to play pool."

WHAT'S ON THE CLUB STEREO?
"At the start of the season it was horrendous, nobody took control and whoever brought in a CD had it played – we even had Frank Sinatra one week! Fortunately, now Kieron [Dyer] is back in the side and he always puts together a mix CD of hip-hop, R&B and even a little bit of Luther Vandross."

YOU'RE IN THE CUP FINAL, THERE'S NOT LONG TO GO, AND A SHOT IS GOING INTO THE TOP CORNER. YOU ARE THE LAST MAN. DO YOU PALM IT AWAY AND GET SENT OFF, OR TRY TO STOP IT LEGITIMATELY?
"I'd try and head it away. If I handled and got sent off, we'd be down to ten men and likely to concede the penalty anyway. But I'd do my best to get to it and hopefully I'd head it back off the bar and away to safety!"

LAST CD YOU BOUGHT?
"Taio Cruz, which is nice and chilled out."

WHAT MUSIC IS IN YOUR CAR?
"Aside from Taio Cruz, on the way to a game, the tempo goes up and I play M People to get me in the mood."

FAVOURITE MEAL?
"I'm a big fan of fajitas as they're simple and easy to cook. I also like a good fillet steak when I'm out, or garlic king prawns. Lovely!"

TAKE YOUR PICK...

PREM OR CHAMPIONS LEAGUE
"Champions League."

BLONDES OR BRUNETTES
"Brunettes."

IPOD OR PLAYSTATION
"iPod."

SOCCER AM OR MOTD
"Soccer AM."

PARTING SHOT

PLAYER FILE

Your guide to the stars and their lifestyles...

THIS MONTH: CRAIG GORDON HEARTS AND SCOTLAND KEEPER

NAME: Craig Gordon.
NICKNAME:
Shania (but a long time ago!)
BIRTHPLACE:
December 31, 1982, Edinburgh.
PREVIOUS CLUBS:
Hearts since youngster.
MARITAL STATUS:
Girlfriend, Jennifer.
CAR: BMW X5
MOBILE PHONE:
Sony Eriksson.

FOOTBALL

BEST MOMENT IN FOOTBALL?
"Winning the Scottish Cup with Hearts last season. Lifting a cup for your club is something you dream about as a boyhood fan, so to do it is very special."

...AND THE WORST?
"Probably being left out of the team this season for five months and not really knowing why. It was great to get back in."

BEST PLAYER YOU'VE FACED?
"Thierry Henry when he played at Hampden against Scotland and we managed to beat France 1-0.

He hit the post from about 30 yards which was a great strike but I saved it coming back off the post so I am claiming it!"

HAS THE BOSS EVER GIVEN YOU A TICKING OFF?
"Once, early in my career, I was taking too long with my kicks for my manager's liking so he chucked the ice bucket at me at half-time and told me to get a move on. That was Craig Levein – get his name in there!"

YOU CAN SIGN ANY PLAYER IN THE WORLD FOR YOUR TEAM...
"Cristiano Ronaldo because we are struggling for right-sided midfield players at the moment and he would fit in quite nicely. He's been phenomenal this season and deserves a whole bunch of awards."

ANY SUPERSTITIONS?
"I've got absolutely hundreds! I think that's a goalkeeper thing but I have another superstition that I can't tell anyone about them... so I can't tell you what they are!

WHO'S THE WORST TRAINER AT THE CLUB?
"Jose Goncalves. He never trains unless he is 100 per cent fit. He spends more time in the medical room than anybody else. If he had a broken finger nail or torn eyelash he would be in there."

AND THE BEST?
"Neil McCann, a top professional and he puts everything into training every day even though he is in his thirties now."

WORST DRESSER AT THE CLUB?
"All the Lithuanians, absolutely horrendous. They come in with the brightest clothes that don't match – green, pink, it doesn't matter, they can all be in the same outfit. Hard to single one of them out but probably Saulius Mikoliunas."

LIFESTYLE

MOST FAMOUS PERSON YOU HAVE EVER MET?
"It's got to be Jimmy Bullard from Fulham... he is a top man, a really funny guy, you just can't stop laughing at him."

FAVOURITE TV PROGRAMME?
"I know it's old, but Friends, I still laugh at it."

WHO'S IN CHARGE OF THE CLUB STEREO AND WHAT DOES HE PLAY?
"The masseur – he owns his own studio and he used to play in a

band so he thinks he has the music sorted but he takes a bit of stick. He plays a whole range but does go back to older stuff and a few of his old singles."

LAST CD YOU BOUGHT?
"Paolo Nutini's These Streets."

WHAT MUSIC IS IN YOUR CAR AT THE MOMENT?
"Paolo Nutini, Kanye West, Black Eyed Peas…"

FAVOURITE MEAL?
"Chinese, a deep fried shredded beef with yeung chow fried rice, very healthy!"

TAKE YOUR PICK...

BLONDES OR BRUNETTES?
"I don't care!"

IPOD OR PLAYSTATION?
"iPod"

RICKY GERVAIS OR PETER KAY?
"Peter Kay."

Craig Gordon wears Under Armour. For more information visit www.underarmour.co.uk

ENGLAND

FACT FILE

MICHAEL OWEN

BIRTH DATE: December 14, 1979

BIRTH PLACE: Chester

POSITION: Striker

HEIGHT: 1.75m (5ft 9in)

CLUBS:
Liverpool, Real Madrid,
Newcastle United, Man United

INTERNATIONAL:
England (89 caps, 40 goals)

DID YOU KNOW?
Michael loves racing and has his
own stables to train racehorses.
The first one he owned was called
Etienne Lady, named after the city
in France where he scored his
famous World Cup goal against
Argentina in 1998.

HOW ENGLAND WERE ROBBED OF THEIR TOP SCORER!

As England fans suffered watching
their side under-perform at the 2010
World Cup finals one supporter
struggled more than most.

Striker Michael Owen - England's
fourth-highest goal scorer of all-
time - was like every other dedicated
follower of the Three Lions in
feeling the hurt and embarrassment
of an under-achieving side.

The arguments had already raged
well before Fabio Capello picked his
final 23-man squad on whether Owen
should be part of the set-up or not.

In the end, all of the debating for
and against the Manchester United
hit-man being included in the
final squad for South Africa was
irrelevant as the player was battling
back from a long-term injury.

When Owen left Newcastle in summer
2009 on a surprise free transfer to Old
Trafford many fans believed it could be
a new dawn for his career. A chance to
prove he had put injury problems behind
him and perhaps even persuade Capello
that he was ready for an England recall.

But events on the pitch overtook the
arguments. The startling form of Wayne
Rooney and boss Sir Alex Ferguson's
decision to play a lot of the time with just
one front man limited Owen's chances.

However, he scored the first in United's
2-1 League Cup victory over Aston Villa
on February 28 and the signs were good.

But then, ironically at the home of
English football, Owen had to be taken
off with a hamstring injury that was
blamed on the state of the Wembley
pitch and his season was over.

OWEN GOAL

The player who had made a name for himself with a wonder-goal against Argentina at the 1998 World Cup would not be able to play in his fourth finals.

Having appeared at France '98, Owen also turned out - and scored two goals - when the tournament arrived in Japan and South Korea in 2002.

He failed to score at Germany 2006 and was injured in the final group game, ruling him out of the game for months.

But he had appeared and scored for the Three Lions at both Euro 2000 and 2004.

That means Owen is still the only English player to hit the back of the net in four major tournaments.

DAWN OF A NEW ERA

With Wayne Rooney off form for the 2010 World Cup finals and England in desperate need of goals they could have done a lot worse than have proven scorer Michael Owen around.

When he left Liverpool for Real Madrid in 2004 Owen was one of the most feared strikers in the Premier League.

In Spain, despite a lack of starting chances, Owen's goals-to-games ratio was up there with the best. His return to the Premier League with Newcastle looked to be yet another forward step in his career – but things went horribly wrong due to a series of crippling injuries.

"I didn't set the world alight in my last year at Newcastle but that is no one's fault but mine. We weren't playing well as a team and I wasn't doing my bit either," he admits.

"I don't believe I am injury prone. You pick up injuries here and there but that is part of the rigours of the modern game. As a footballer you always get the chance to have the last laugh and

I'm totally confident about the future. I can do my talking on the pitch."

Owen admits he jumped at the chance of joining the Red Devils: "I want to replay Sir Alex for showing faith in me and I gave him my assurance I will repay him with goals and my performances. I was always clinging to the hope that one day he would ask me to come and play for them."

He may not have had the number of appearances he had hoped for during his first few months at Old Trafford but a Champions League hat-trick against Wolfsburg and the winner in the Manchester derby cemented a place in United history.

But he wants a lot more. "I am hungry to do well. If this challenge doesn't put a spring in your step and a smile on your face then nothing will. I don't think I need to prove anything to people who have asked if I am hungry."

Owen points out: "I've played more than 500 games at the highest level for clubs and with England, so I can't have been on the treatment table all of the time."

Even as he approaches his 31st birthday, it's still far too early to write off Michael Owen.

➲ HIS BOSS SAYS

Sir Alex Ferguson
Manchester United Manager

"Michael Owen is one of the very best strikers around in terms of his positional play and finishing. You can't dismiss his record. His record for England is outstanding."

➲ MICHAEL'S MAGIC MARKERS

1997: Premier League debut and Liverpool's top-scorer (as he would be every year until 2004).

1998: England's youngest-ever player and youngest-ever scorer; PFA Young Player of the Year; Premier League Golden Boot; BBC Sports Personality of the Year.

1999: Premier League Golden Boot

2001: European Footballer of the Year; First player since Sir Geoff Hurst in 1966 to score a hat-trick against Germany.

CLASSIC IMAGE

WE WERE THERE... MICHAEL OWEN, ENGLAND

Michael Owen is a true professional - on the pitch, on the ball, in front of goal and in front of the camera! Just before the 2002 finals in Japan and South Korea, the striker agreed to be the face of **Shoot's** World Cup Special. We got him posing sitting on a stool in the stockroom of the sports shop at Wigan's Soccer Centre and took along one of the brand new England shirts for him to wear. No messing about for hours in front of a camera with Michael - he'd pulled off the right poses in less than ten minutes, both with and without the Three Lions shirt. And all that after he had just filmed a television advert for a breakfast cereal!

WE WERE THERE...
PAOLO DICANIO, WEST HAM

Paolo di Canio had arranged his meeting with **Shoot** months earlier but come the day of the interview he didn't feel like chatting. The loopy Italian claimed his tummy ached after training and wasn't sure about chatting. It was, of course, total rubbish. He just loved a bit more attention and once he got chatting there was no stopping him! No question dodging from the eccentric forward as he stood inside West Ham's indoor training centre at Chadwell Heath in Essex. And when it came to the picture session he was equally animated agreeing to pull faces and gestures for the cameraman, pose in the Hammers soon-to-be-released shirt and even pretend he was behind bars! He then made his excuses and left – he said he had to go home and feed the fish! Honestly! We didn't believe it either, but later found out he kept piranahs!

CLASSIC IMAGE

MAICON
BRAZIL'S RAIDING RIGHT-BACK

There's nothing quite like watching a full-back who gallops down the outside of the pitch like a winger and is able and willing to ping in great crosses.

If the defender can also score goals he can become an instant hit with fans. Say hello to Brazil's Maicon!

He's built like a tank but moves like a high-speed train. Not only does he look like a formidable opponent – he actually is one!

Maicon has managed to keep Danni Alves out of the Brazil side, which says all you need to know about his ability. But he is also rated highly off the pitch by former international boss Dunga who says the player is a massive influence in the dressing room.

Maicon also has an eye for the spectacular as anyone who saw his goal against North Korea at South Africa 2010 will agree.

From an incredible angle, virtually on the line, he managed to somehow get the ball past the keeper and into the back of the next.

Was it a shot or was it a fluke? It was a shot! He scored a similar goal against Portugal in 2008 and go back a further four years to the 2004 Olympics and there he sailed past five defenders to score another memorable goal.

FACT FILE

Name:
Maicon Douglas Sisenando
Position: Right-back
Birth place:
Novo Hamburgo, Brazil
Birth date: July 26, 1981
Height: 1.84m (6ft)
Clubs:
Cruzeiro, Monaco,
Inter Milan
Joined Inter Milan:
July 2006
Transfer fee:
Would cost £25m

WORLD CUP 2010

Games: 5
Minutes played: 450
Goals: 1
Bookings: 0
Man of the Match:
Brazil v North Korea

HIGUAIN
ARGENTINA'S LIVEWIRE STRIKER

Gonzalo Higuain will forever be remembered for his hat-trick against South Korea at World Cup 2010.

As his Argentina team progressed thanks to those goals, the side he could have been playing for were on their way home.

Higuain was born in France and for a number of years they wanted him to play for them. But he was determined to turn out for the birth country of his father Jorge.

Amazingly for such a talented player, Higuain had never appeared at international level for any country until he turned out in the Argentines' Olympic side in 2008 and their Under-23 side in 2009 for a friendly.

Just months after that one-minute appearance for the Under-23 team he was called up by Argentina coach Diego Maradona for a World Cup qualifier against Peru – and promptly scored.

His hat-trick at South Africa 2010 made him only the third Argentina player to get three in World Cup finals and the first player since 2002 to grab a trio in the tournament's final stages.

Real Madrid have tied him down with a contract to 2016 – no surprise after he scored 28 La Liga goals for them in season 2009-10 and 31 the previous campaign.

And don't forget his 11 Champions League strikes over that same period!

FACT FILE
Name: Gonzalo Higuain
Position: Striker
Birth place: Brest, France
Birth date: December 19, 1987
Height: 1.85m (6ft 1in)
Clubs:
River Plate, Real Madrid
Joined Real Madrid:
January 2007
Transfer fee:
£8.5m

WORLD CUP 2010
Games: 4
Minutes played: 341
Goals: 4
Bookings: 0
Man of the Match:
Argentina v South Korea

ROBBEN
HOLLAND'S WING MAESTRO

Arjen Robben had made quite a name for himself in Holland before he arrived at Chelsea for £12m in 2004.

Although he played his part in helping the Blues to two Premier League titles, his time in the Premier League was punctuated by injury.

But Spanish giant Real Madrid had seen enough during Robben's three years at Stamford Bridge to pay double what Chelsea had forked out to get the Dutchman's signature.

Robben did little wrong at the Bernabeau and played a vital part in Madrid's side once he had earned his first-team place.

But the £80m arrival of Cristiano Ronaldo and £56m move of Kaka meant players had to be off-loaded.

Robben was sold to Bayern Munich for £22m in August 2009 and scored two goals on his Bundesliga debut which helped towards his side winning the 2009-10 title.

That was five league titles in just eight years for the player, highlighting his value to his various clubs.

Robben's speed makes him a danger but opposition defenders also find it difficult to cope with his trickery. He is also effective as a striker.

FACT FILE
Name:
Arjen Robben
Position:
Winger
Birth place:
Bedum, Holland
Birth date:
January 23, 1984
Height:
1.8m (5ft 11in)
Clubs: Groningen, PSV
Eindhoven, Chelsea,
Real Madrid, Bayern Munich
Joined Bayern:
August 2009
Transfer fee:
£22m

WORLD CUP 2010
Games: 5
Minutes played: 387
Goals: 2
Bookings: 2
Man of the Match:
Holland v Slovakia

FABIANO
THE HIT-MAN FROM BRAZIL

It wasn't until he arrived in Spain that Luis Fabiano started to realise his true potential – and create a name for himself in Europe.

With a goal virtually every other game for Sevilla, Fabiano has become one of their key players and has probably tripled his value during his time with the club.

Quick and powerful with a lethal strike, he's noted for scoring spectacular goals – the mark of a natural goal-scorer.

Brazil gave him his debut in 2003 but the player struggled to make a starting place his own until 2007.

During the qualifiers for South Africa 2010 he excelled, ensuring his place in the country's final squad.

Second top scorer in his qualification group, during the same period he also added the Golden Ball for top marksman at the Confederations Cup.

FACT FILE

Name:
Luis Fabiano Clemente
Position:
Striker
Birth place:
Campinas, Brazil
Birth date:
November 8, 1980
Height:
1.83m (6ft)
Clubs:
Ponte Preta, Rennes, Sao Paolo, Porto, Sevilla
Joined Sevilla:
July 2005
Transfer fee:
Could cost £20m

WORLD CUP 2010

Games: 5
Minutes played: 418
Goals: 3
Bookings: 1
Man of the Match:
Brazil v Ivory Coast

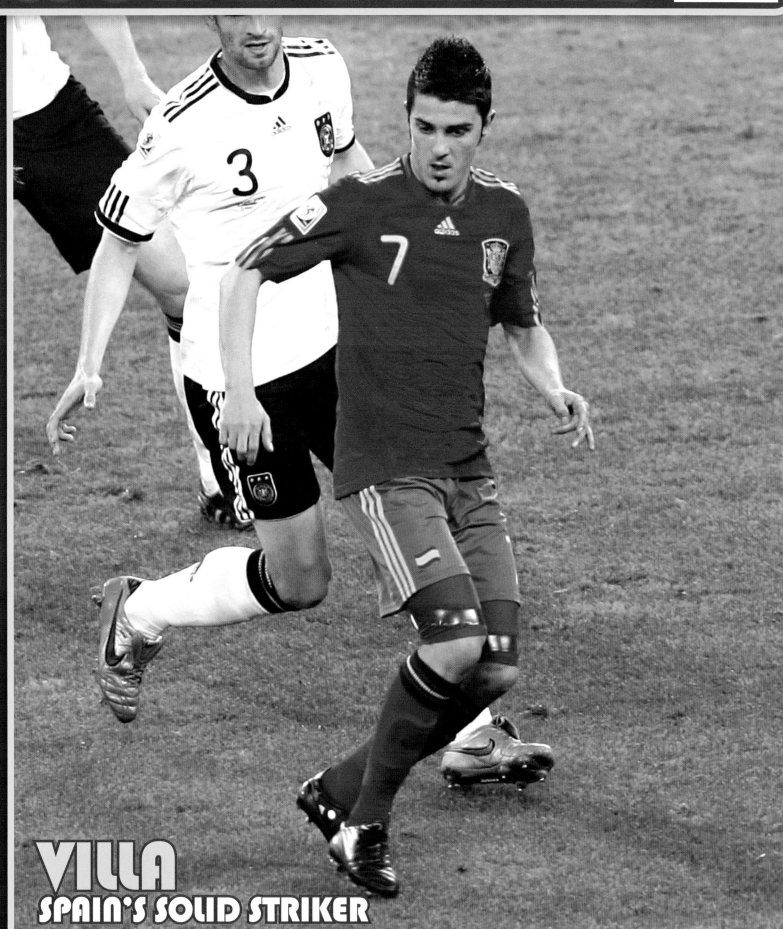

VILLA
SPAIN'S SOLID STRIKER

One half of Spain's deadly duo with Fernando Torres, David Villa has an incredible goal-scoring record.

His 107 goals in 166 league games for Valencia persuaded Barcelona to fork out £30m for him at the end of the 2009-10 season.

Barca will have also noticed his record of a goal every game and half for his country, which has elevated him to legendary status with quite a bit of his career still in front of him.

Villa has worn the legendary No.7 shirt - once on the back of Raul - for Spain and that has done nothing to quieten the comparisons between the two prolific strikers.

Villa will have overtaken Raul as his country's top scorer by the time you read this, his strike rate per game already the third best in Spain's history.

Whether he plays his usual role as a main striker, behind a frontman or wide left, Villa has only one thing in his sights - the back of the net!

He's quick off the mark and committed but like most highly rated forwards he's not afraid to put in a hard shift and help out the midfield when they are under pressure.

FACT FILE

Name:
David Villa Sanchez
Position:
Striker
Birth place:
Langreo, Spain
Birth date:
December 3, 1981
Height:
1.75m (5ft 9in)
Clubs:
Sporting Gijon, Zaragoza, Valencia, Barcelona
Joined Barcelona: May 2010
Transfer fee: £30m

WORLD CUP 2010

Games: 7
Minutes played: 635
Goals: 5
Bookings: 0
Man of the Match:

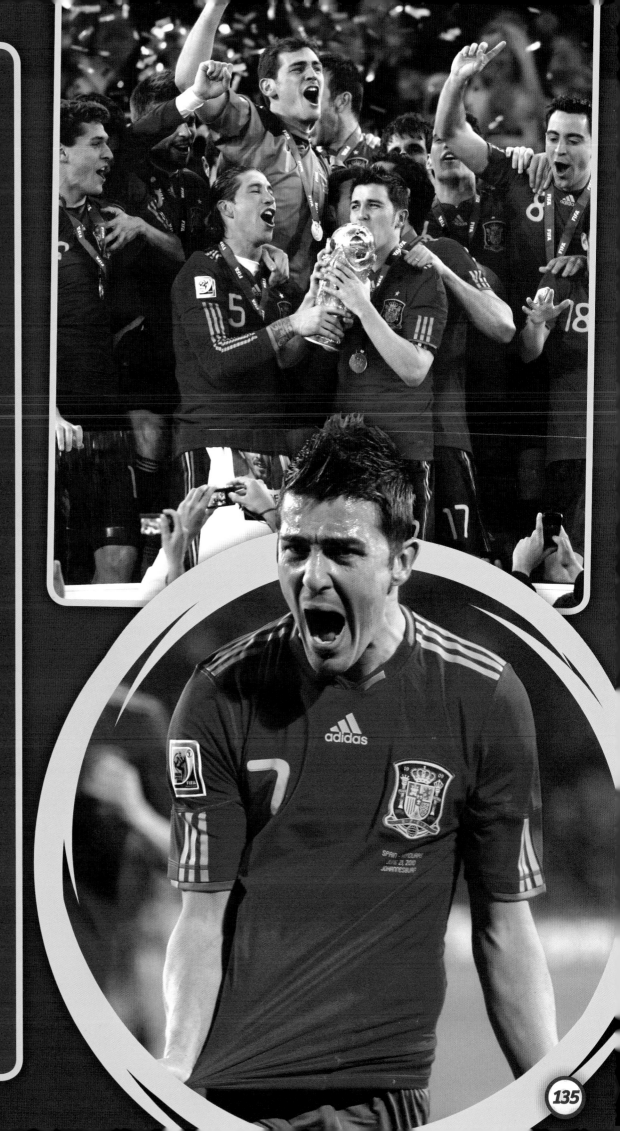

MULLER
GERMANY'S MIDFIELD MAGICIAN

England fans have every right to hate Thomas Muller. He stunned the Three Lions with two goals in the 4-1 World Cup demolition by Germany.

But a lot of players are hated because they are good - and would be welcomed at their clubs with open arms by those same detractors!

Muller is one such player. After just one full season with Bayern Munich's first-team he's become a vital attacking cog in their machine.

He only made his full Germany international debut in March 2010, just three months before the World Cup finals, although he had represented his country at various levels since the age of 16 and was established at Under-21 level.

A scorer and creator of goals he has pace and skill and can operate as an attacking midfielder or in any of the forward line roles.

But he's not just a good footballer - he's been classed as intelligent, bubbly and reliable by his team-mates who are hoping that his contract will be extended beyond the 2013 that has already been agreed.

At the age of 20 he's already got a Bundesliga title under his belt, along with a German Cup winner's medal and was in the Bayern side beaten by Inter Milan in the 2010 Champions League Final.

FACT FILE
Name: Thomas Muller
Position: Midfielder
Birth place:
Weilheim, Germany
Birth date:
September 13, 1989
Height: 1.86m (6ft 1in)
Clubs: Bayern Munich
Joined Bayern Munich: 2000
Transfer fee:
Would be worth £12m

WORLD CUP 2010
Games: 6
Minutes played: 473
Goals: 5
Bookings: 2
Man of the Match:
Uruguay v Germany
Germany v England

20 QUESTIONS

TO TEST YOUR FOOTBALL KNOWLEDGE!

You think you know all there is to know about football? Here's your chance to prove it with 20 questions about your favourite sport. Some maybe easy, some are difficult and some will be trick questions...

1

Who scored England's first goal at South Africa 2010?

A. DEFOE

B. HESKEY

C. GERRARD

2

Who is England's most-capped player?

A. DAVID BECKHAM

B. PETER SHILTON

C. BOBBY CHARLTON

3

Which country does Gonzalo Higuain play for?

A. ARGENTINA

B. BRAZIL

C. ITALY

4

Who was England manager at World Cup 2006?

A. FABIO CAPELLO

B. STEVE MCCLAREN

C. SVEN GORAN ERIKSSON

6

Michael Owen scored a hat-trick for England in 2001 against which side?

A. ARGENTINA

B. LUXEMBOURG

C. GERMANY

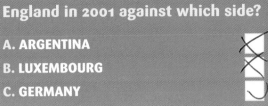

7

FOREST

Who was the manager who won two European titles with Nottingham Forest?

A. BILL SHANKLY

B. BOBBY ROBSON

C. BRIAN CLOUGH

5

In what year did Sir Alex Ferguson take over as Manchester United boss?

A. 1986

B. 1991

C. 1999

8

After he left Man United, George Best played for which side?

A. FULHAM

B. LUTON

C. QPR

10

What shirt number did Kenny Dalglish wear at Liverpool?

A. NUMBER 7

B. NUMBER 9

C. NUMBER 10

9

Who was the first black player to turn out for England?

A. PAUL INCE   B. VIV ANDERSON   C. ANDY COLE

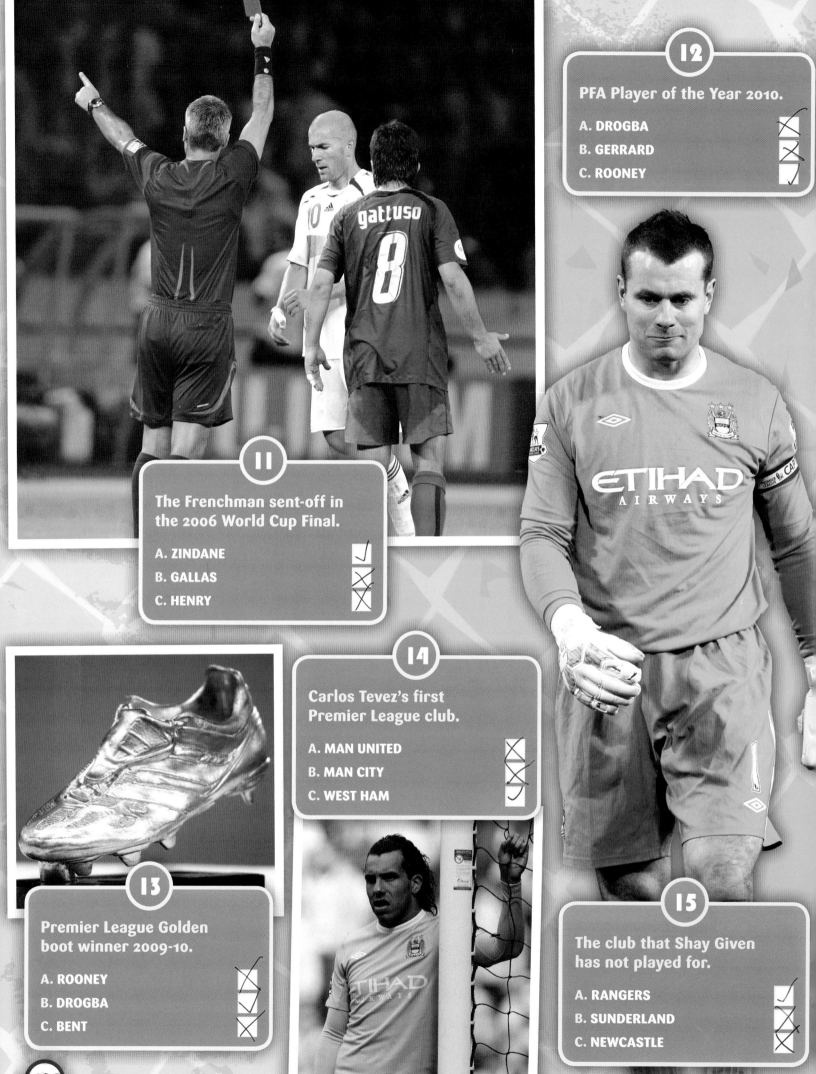

12

PFA Player of the Year 2010.

A. DROGBA

B. GERRARD

C. ROONEY

11

The Frenchman sent-off in the 2006 World Cup Final.

A. ZINDANE ✓

B. GALLAS ✗

C. HENRY ✗

14

Carlos Tevez's first Premier League club.

A. MAN UNITED ✗

B. MAN CITY ✗

C. WEST HAM ✗

13

Premier League Golden boot winner 2009-10.

A. ROONEY

B. DROGBA ✗

C. BENT ✗

15

The club that Shay Given has not played for.

A. RANGERS ✓

B. SUNDERLAND

C. NEWCASTLE ✗

141

17

How many players have captained England in World Cup finals games?

A. 10

B. 9

C. 8

18

The number of Scotland caps won by Kenny Dalglish.

A. 92

B. 102

C. 112

16

Paolo Di Canio's club when he was sent off for pushing the ref.

A. WEST HAM UNITED ✓

B. SHEFFIELD UNITED ✗

C. SHEFFIELD WEDNESDAY ✗

19

Dino Zoff's age when he last won a World Cup with Italy.

A. 37 ✗

B. 40 ✗

C. 41 ✓

20

The club Fernando Torres played for before joining Liverpool.

A. VILLARREALL ✗

B. REAL MADRID ✗

C. ATLETICO MADRID ✓